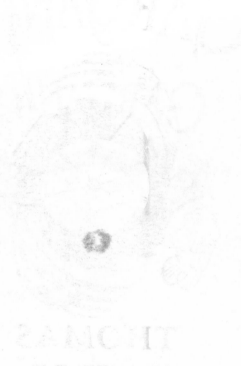

GARGANTIS

THOMAS TAYLOR

WITH ILLUSTRATIONS BY THE AUTHOR

WALKER BOOKS

First published 2020 by Walker Books Ltd
87 Vauxhall Walk, London SE11 5HJ

2 4 6 8 10 9 7 5 3 1

This book has been typeset in Stempel Schneider

Printed and bound by CPI Group (UK) Ltd, Croydon CR0 4YY

British Library Cataloguing in Publication Data:
a catalogue record for this book is available from the British Library

ISBN 978-1-4063-8629-5 (Trade)
ISBN 978-1-4063-9661-4 (Exclusive)

www.walker.co.uk

For Max ～ *T.T.*

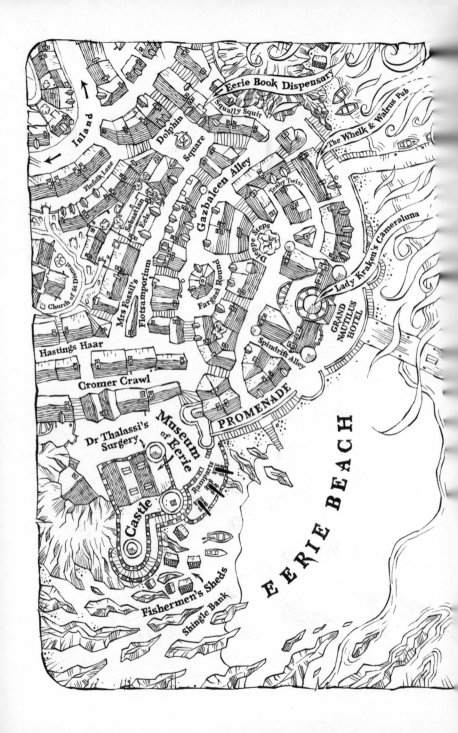

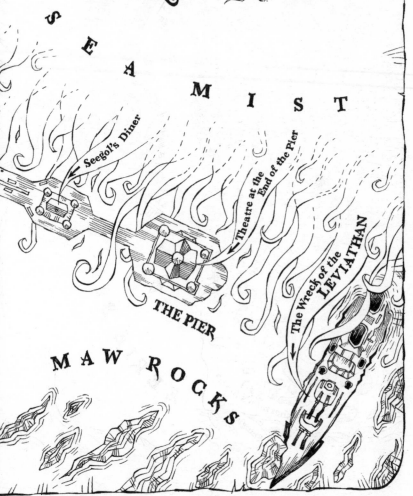

MAP
of
EERIE -on- SEA

S E A   M I S T

Harbour Wall

Seegol's Diner

Theatre at the End of the Pier

The Wreck of the LEVIATHAN

THE PIER

M A W   R O C K S

DEEP HOOD

IF THERE'S ONE THING hotels have a lot of, it's strangers. Hotels are kind of in the stranger business, after all. But no hotel in the world puts the *strange* in *stranger* quite like the Grand Nautilus Hotel.

Take this guy, for example. The one who's just come in from the storm. The one walking across the empty marble floor of the lobby. See him? The one whose face is hidden by the enormous hood of a long waxed coat streaming with rainwater? He doesn't even pull his hood back to talk to the receptionist, and his luggage – a metal-bound wooden box clutched in one gloved hand – doesn't leave his side for a moment.

Who is he? What's his story?

What's in the box?

Of course, we'll probably never know. And that's fine. People are entitled to their privacy. Privacy is something else hotels have a lot of. Besides, there's something sinister about this man, something threatening that makes me *not want* to know, to be honest. I'll be quite happy once he's up in his room, doing whatever dark and secret things he's come here to do, far away from me. He takes his key and steps away from the reception desk ...

... and starts walking in my direction!

I sit up and adjust my cap.

"May I help you, sir?" I say as the man in the overlong coat stops before the desk of my little cubbyhole. I look up and see nothing but darkness in that drooping hood. My cap starts to slip down the back of my head, so I straighten it.

"Herbert Lemon." A voice comes from inside the hood, and I flinch. There's an unnatural edge to that voice that makes my skin crawl.

"Th-that's right, sir," I reply. "I'm Herbie Lemon, Lost-and-Founder at the Grand Nautilus Hotel, at your service. Have you lost something?"

There's a sudden *KER-KER-BOOM!* as a clap of thunder gallops around the town outside. The flash of lightning that rides with it only serves to highlight the darkness in the man's hood. The wind flings rain against the windowpanes, and the hotel lamps flicker.

The man remains motionless, dripping rainwater on my counter.

"U-u-umbrella, perhaps?" I suggest.

I glance at the metal-bound box in the man's hand. There's barely room for a change of underpants in a thing like that.

"Or luggage, maybe?"

My voice is almost a squeak now.

The man leans in, his hood nearly closing over my head. My nostrils fill with the stink of wet coat and fishy breath.

"Do not ask what I have lost, Herbert Lemon," comes the man's voice, sounding as if each word is made with a great deal of effort. "Ask what I have found."

And that's when there's another crash of thunder and the hotel's lights go out.

Now, I know what you're thinking. Yes, you – sitting there safe at home, staring into your book with bug eyes, waiting for something horrible to happen to me. You're thinking that I'm going to freak out now. And I admit, I am considering it. But you don't get to be Lost-and-Founder at the Grand Nautilus Hotel without learning how to be a professional. So, OK, yes, maybe I'm not the bravest mouse in the basket, but I am in *my* place, behind *my* polished desk, master of *my* own little world of lost property and shiny buttons. And so that's why, when the lights come back on again, I'm still sitting exactly where I was, clutching my Lost-and-Founder's cap with both hands and … blinking at empty space.

Because, of course, the man with the deep hood has gone.

WEIRDOS AND CRACKPOTS

THE SECOND RULE of lost-and-foundering is: *Keep calm and try a smile.*

Seriously, you'd be amazed at some of the things that turn up in my Lost-and-Foundery: thingummies, doodahs, assorted hoojamfips of all descriptions. Once, I even had a living, breathing human being hand herself in, but that's another story. You just have to take it all in your stride, stay cool and pretend that the Roman helmet, or false nostril, or bloodstained candlestick that got left in the conservatory is all in a day's work for a Lost-and-Founder. So it's the second rule I'm mostly thinking of when the hotel lights come back on to reveal that not only has Deep Hood gone, he's also left an object on my desk.

"You were just handing something in?" I ask the

empty space where the man had been standing. "Why did you have to be so creepy about it?"

I lean out of my cubbyhole and see a trail of rainwater leading to the main staircase. If I wanted to, I could follow it and find out which room Deep Hood's staying in.

If I wanted to.

And the thing on my desk? Well, see for yourself.

It's a shell.

A strange, spiky shell – pearly white and spiralling around itself until it ends in a point. The small spikes, which are slightly curved, run up this spiral at regular intervals. I pick up the shell and peer into the trumpet end (it's one of those sorts of shells). It seems heavier than it should be, and it gives a clear metallic tinkle when I shake it. There's a small hole in one side, rimmed with brass. Is there something inside? Cautiously, I put the shell to my ear.

"I can hear the sea," I say to myself with a nervous chuckle of relief. "That means it's empty, right?"

"Or your head is," says an annoying voice, and I nearly drop the shell in surprise. From behind a large potted fern near my cubbyhole steps Mr Mollusc, the hotel manager. He takes the shell from me.

"Shiny thing." His eyes light up. "Probably worth

quite a bit. What are you doing with something like this, Lemon?"

"It was handed in, sir," I say. "By that new guest."

At this, old Mollusc's horrible moustache bristles, and he almost throws the shell back to me.

"You spoke to him?" he says, nodding fearfully at the stairs. "He spoke to you?"

I shrug and hope that's answer enough.

Mollusc runs his fingers through his thinning hair.

"Why do we always get the strangest ones?" he asks, though mostly to himself.

I shrug again.

I mean, surely he knows the answer to *that* by now. Summer is a faded memory, and Eerie-on-Sea hasn't pretended to be a normal seaside town for so long that I wonder if it'll remember how when the tourists return. Winter is lingering, and a storm mightier than any I have ever seen has engulfed the bay, turning the sea into a raging animal and blowing winds that would strip the enamel from your teeth. Only weirdos and crackpots would travel all the way to Eerie-on-Sea at this time of year. And where else are those weirdos and crackpots going to stay but the Grand Nautilus Hotel?

"Er, did *you* speak to him, sir?" I say, daring a question

of my own. "His voice was a bit … you know. Did you think his voice was a bit … you know?"

"Don't be impertinent!" snaps Mr Mollusc, suddenly remembering himself. "You have a new piece of lost property to take care of, boy. No doubt of great value. Kindly get on with your job."

And with that he turns on his heel and strides away.

Across the lobby, Amber Griss – the hotel receptionist – gives me a smile that seems to say, "Oh, don't mind him, Herbie. You know what he's like." But her raised eyebrow adds, "Just don't let him see you making that face!" So I grin an "Oops! You're right!" grin back and lift down the heavy old ledger instead.

This ledger is where I, and all the Lost-and-Founders before me, record everything that is handed in at the Lost-and-Foundery, as well as everything that is successfully returned. It's enormous. I heave it open and flip to the next blank space. I write the time and date and then the words PECULIAR SHELL. I'm not quite sure what else to write, to be honest.

Some of the hotel's clocks, the faster ones, start chiming for 7 p.m. It's been a long day, so I just write, INVESTIGATION BEGUN AT 7-ISH next to PECULIAR SHELL. Then I close the ledger with a thud, flip the sign on my desk to CLOSED, and carry the strange shell down to my cellar.

The cellar is the real heart of the Lost-and-Foundery: a whole wing of the hotel's basement that generations of Lost-and-Founders have called home and that has long since become a glittering cavern of curiosities. Someone once described it as "Aladdin's cave", but it's not.

It's mine.

I shove a log into my little wood burner, hang my cap on a curly bronze whatsit and flop down into my enormous armchair. The gale whistles through the chimney, and the walls quake with an almighty thunderclap, but the storm can't reach me down here. I grab my largest magnifying glass – itself a lost item – and use it to turn my eye enormous as I peer closely at the curious shell. In particular at the small brass-lined hole.

"Something interesting?" comes a voice, and for the second time the shell nearly flies out of my hand, as I start in surprise.

"Can people please stop doing that?" I shout as the shadows move and Violet Parma steps into the firelight to sit beside me. She's holding a large white cat.

"Doing what?" she asks.

"Jumping out! I was just thinking how this place is

mine-all-mine, and then you pop up from behind the lost pyjamas and spoil it."

"You did say I could come around whenever I wanted," says Violet with a slight lift of her chin. "And there was a time when you invited me to live down here, remember?"

And both those things are true, even if the second one turned out a bit differently in the end.

But wait, you're probably wondering who Violet Parma is. Unless you've been to Eerie-on-Sea before, that is, and have heard all the stories about her. And if *that's* the case, then let me tell you that those stories are also true. I know because I was there for most of them. But whatever you've heard, and whatever I say, and whatever you think of this wild-haired, brown-eyed girl with a cat, all that really matters right now is that Violet is my best friend here in Eerie, and she knows how to open my cellar window.

"Besides," says Violet, "the storm is worse than ever. Poor Erwin here got lifted right off his paws and was nearly swept out to sea! I didn't think you'd mind us hiding out down here for a while." And she puts Erwin – that's the cat, by the way – in his favourite box of lost scarves, the one I keep near the wood burner.

"You've got something new," Violet adds, staring eagerly at the iridescent shell in my hands.

"There's a hole in the side." I flip the shell around. "I was just going to look in it, to see—"

"Great idea!" Violet takes the shell and the magnifying glass from me, and now she's the one with the giant eye, peering into the hole in the shell.

"There *is* something in there!" she cries.

"What sort of something?" I ask, deciding not to protest.

"In the bottom of the hole." Violet's eye looks bigger than ever as she leans into the magnifying lens. "There's a piece of metal, like a little pin with squared-off sides. The kind of thing you see when you look into the winding hole of an old-fashioned clock."

"Like the kind of thing that's turned with a key?"

"Exactly," says Violet. "You have some of those keys, don't you? Herbie, I think there's clockwork in this shell!"

I open the large toolbox beside my repair desk, heave out a big jar and carefully tip its contents into the pool of light from my anglepoise lamp. From the jar spills keys of every kind. It takes a bit of poking about, but eventually I find a brass winder key that neatly fits the hole in the shell.

"Well?" says Violet when I don't turn the key. "What are you waiting for?"

"Maybe we shouldn't," I reply. My mind goes back to the creepy man who left this shell, with his disturbing voice and drooping hood. "I'm supposed to keep things safe, Vi, not mess around with them. Maybe it wouldn't be right to wind this thing up."

"Are you serious?" Violet blinks at me. "How can you not be curious to see what it does?"

"I am curious, but…"

I glance over towards Erwin and see that the cat, while in every other way appearing to be fast asleep, has one ice-blue eye wide open and is staring at us intently. It looks as though Erwin is on Violet's side, as usual.

"I just wonder if…"

"Oh, give it to me." Violet takes the shell again.

She turns the key.

SEA SHANTY

VIOLET GIVES THE KEY three sharp turns...

Tic-tic-tic-TIK, tic-tic-tic-TIK, tic-tic-tic-TIK.

Nothing happens.

She puts the spiky shell down on the table beside my chair.

Nothing continues to happen.

"Wait," she says. "Can you hear that? It's doing *something*."

I stretch my hearing, and yes, sure enough, there's a faint whirring from inside the shell, as if tiny gears are moving into position.

Then the shell stands up.

Or rather, it pops up a finger's width above the table as a small brass arm reaches down from the trumpet end and elevates the shell. Then music starts – a tinkling tune that dances in the air as the shell begins to rotate on the brass arm, sending points of reflected lamplight flickering across the arched ceiling of my cellar.

"It's beautiful!" gasps Violet. "And the tune seems familiar…"

"It should," I say. "It's a sea shanty."

"A what?"

"A sea shanty. You know, one of the songs the fishermen sing. You must have heard them when they're hauling their fishing boats up the beach, or doing fishy things on the harbour wall. They're always singing."

"It sounds different like this, though," says Violet. "Prettier. More magical."

The music ends, and the shell stops spinning. It sinks back down onto the table.

"So, it's a music box," I say, thinking I should add this fact to the ledger. "That might make it easier to find its rightful owner…"

The shell stands up again.

And I mean REALLY stands up this time, on four little brass legs – each like the leg of a crab – which pop out from inside it with a metallic *CLACK!* Violet and I, who had been leaning in close to hear the music, start back in surprise. Even Erwin sits up in his box of scarves and gives a hiss of alarm. The shell pivots my way, as if looking at me, though there's no eye that I can see. Then it pivots towards Violet. A fifth brass appendage emerges, this time with a tiny pair of scissors attached to the end like a crab claw. The arm waves between us, the little scissors *snip, snip, snip*-ing in a way I can only describe as menacing.

"Pass me that bucket," I say to Vi as quietly as I can.

"Why?" comes her reply. "Do you feel sick?"

"No," I mumble. "The third rule of lost-and-foundering. I was forgetting it. Pass me the bucket. Quick!"

Violet reaches over and picks up an old wooden bucket filled with coat hangers. I snatch it from her, tip the coat hangers on the floor and dive towards the shell.

Too late! The thing must sense me somehow, or maybe it's just bad timing, because the shell leaps from the table just as I bring the bucket down, and it scuttles away across the floor. I dive after it, miss again and have to watch helplessly as the little clockwork hermit crab – because that's exactly what it looks like to me – runs up the side of my lost-books bookcase and skitters away along the top. In desperation, I throw the bucket at the shell, knocking it to the ground.

Violet darts forward holding an old woolly jumper and jumps on the shell. She wrestles with it in the jumper for a moment, and I can hear metallic clacking and whirring sounds as the mechanical hermit crab tries to untangle itself. Then the jumper goes still.

"Got it!" she says.

"Do you think it's all wound down now?"

Violet shrugs.

"It's stopped struggling, at least."

"Maybe." I take the jumper from her, careful not to let our little clockwork prisoner escape. "But I'm not taking any chances. If someone comes to claim this wind-up shell, I don't want to have to admit that it's run away and is living wild and free somewhere in my Lost-and-Foundery. Besides, I didn't like the look of those scissors."

I scrunch the jumper – shell and all – into the bucket, place the bucket on the floor upside down, and then put a couple of heavy books on top. If the mechanical contraption still has some wound spring left, that should stop it going anywhere.

"What is it, then?" says Violet.

"A clockwork hermit crab."

"No, I mean the third rule of lost-and-foundering. What's that?"

"The third rule," I say, giving her one of my most impressive looks, "is: *Unexpect the expected!*"

"Shouldn't that be the other way around?"

"Ha!" I reply. "That's just what I unexpected you to say."

"OK." Vi rolls her eyes. "Where did you get that shell from, anyway?"

"Handed in." I flop back into my chair. "New guest, just arrived. He must have found it, um, somewhere."

"You don't know?" says Vi, sitting on the other side of the wood burner. "Didn't you ask where he found it? Didn't you ask for *details*? That's not like you."

I think about explaining, about telling Vi just how weird and sinister the faceless guest was, with his dripping hood and creepy voice, but I can't be bothered. This is mostly because, annoyingly, Violet's right – I should have run after Deep Hood to find out more. How else am I going to return the stupid shell to its rightful owner if I don't follow up leads when they're hot? I'll just have to knock on the man's door in the morning and ask. Right now, though, I'd really like to change the subject, so I'm pleased when Violet changes it for me.

"Are you hungry?" she says. "It's been ages since we last went to Seegol's for fish and chips."

At the mention of Seegol's delicious chips, my stomach does a little flip of anticipation. My ears, however, report the sound of raging weather to my brain, so my brain sends a signal to my stomach to knock it off. My stomach does another little flip anyway.

"I'd love to go," I say. "But the storm…"

"It's a monster," Vi admits with a whistle. "Though it's also exciting to be out in. I've never experienced anything like it. And besides, Seegol's isn't far."

Well, that's true enough, as you'll know if you've ever seen a map of Eerie-on-Sea. But being out on the deck of the pier in this wind, with lightning forking overhead…

"Come on, Herbie!" says Vi, jumping up. "It'll be like we're on an adventure again."

"OK." I stand up and reach for my coat. My firelit corner of the cellar suddenly looks cosier than ever. "And if the storm's really bad, we can always bring the chips back here."

I don't so much climb out of the cellar window as get sucked out. The wind seems to be trying to lift me into the air by my cheeks. I brace myself against it, planting my feet, and see Violet braced too, her mass of dark curls standing out from the sides of her head like a windswept hedge. I start to speak, but a gust of air whips the words away and tries to take my tonsils, too, so I clamp my mouth shut and think of chips. We stumble across the cobbles to the sea wall and squint in astonishment at the sight beyond.

The ocean is devouring the pier.

Or rather, it's trying to: waves like the jaws of some immense, elemental creature chomp at its Victorian ironwork, breaking in gouts of spray that lick the shuddering deck. Garlands of suspended pier lights dance crazily in the wind, while the neon sign – the one that says EERIE-ON-SEA in fizzing, candy-coloured letters – crackles and blinks more than ever. Above this boils the storm in a vault of bruise-coloured clouds, lit with electrical flashes of its own.

Only the lights of Seegol's Diner – the fish and chip shop at the heart of the pier – shine solid and reassuring.

I look at Vi, and her eyes are bright with excitement. She starts down the steps to the pier, clutching the sea wall, then stops. She opens her coat like a pair of wings, waits for them to fill with the furious air and then, at just the right moment …

… she jumps!

Incredibly, the storm holds her in the air, even

lifting her slightly. Violet Parma is flying!

Then gravity notices and drags her back down. Violet lands smartly on the deck of the pier, closes her coat against the buffeting of the storm and beckons me to do the same.

I spread my coat open and look up into the lightning sky. For a moment, I feel like Batman.

Then I see something.

A shape – a colossal, heaving shadow, vaster than imagining – coils through the storm clouds above Eerie-on-Sea.

"!" I cry, all thoughts of Batman swept away.

The wind, as if seeing me miss my chance to fly, punches me back against the sea wall, pinning me there like a curious specimen, hammering my face with spray. It takes a great effort to peel myself off the wall and get my coat closed. I stumble down the steps to join Violet. She's trying not to laugh.

I squint up into the sky and rub my eyes. There's nothing there now but flickering clouds and a tumbling storm. Surely that was all there ever was.

Violet grabs my arm and pulls me along the trembling pier towards Seegol's Diner.

WEATHER-PICKLED REGULARS

WE HAVE TO BATTLE against the gale to get the door of Seegol's open, and when we finally slip inside, the wind slams it shut behind us.

"Ah, such bravery!" comes an accented voice we know well, and Mr Seegol salutes us from behind his counter. This counter is also his kitchen – an island of brushed steel, hissing fryers and warm light, surrounded on all sides by tables and chairs. There are a few people sitting there – weather-pickled regulars who will not let a "bit of a blow" keep them from their golden-fried fish and pots of strong tea. Outside the diner the storm rages as if insulted by all this, clawing at the windows and howling like a banshee around the door.

We sit at a table and breathe in the comforting aroma

of freshly fried chips as Seegol makes his way over.

"Isn't it incredible?" he says.

"The weather?" I reply.

"Of course, the weather!" Seegol cries. "Look at the sea, Herbie! Now is supposed to be low tide, but the wind is so strong it has blown the sea back *up* again!"

As if to prove this, the whole diner leans one way, then the other, making all the salt and pepper pots dance across the tabletops.

"You must have seen storms before," says Violet, clutching her chair. "Living out here on the pier. It's always been a shaky old place."

Seegol wags his finger.

"Never like this," he says, and suddenly I notice that behind his usual cheery exterior, there is a hint of real worry. "Days it has lasted already, and it just seems to grow stronger! And sometimes, when I look up into the clouds, I see... I think I see..."

"What do you see?" I ask.

Seegol looks as if he's about to say one thing but decides instead to say something else.

"Ah, it is nothing. It's hard to see anything straight when Gargantis wakes."

"Gigantic *what* wakes?" I almost manage not to squeak.

But Seegol is staring at the streaming windows, lost in thought, so Violet answers for him.

"When *Gargantis* wakes," she explains. "It's an old Eerie saying. The fishermen use it when there's really bad weather. *Gargantis* is just a local word meaning 'storm'."

"How do you know that?" I'm surprised at Violet telling *me* something about Eerie-on-Sea. She's only been here a few months.

"I read it in a book," she replies, looking pleased with herself.

"Gargantis sleeps, Eerie keeps," says Seegol then, as if he's quoting something. *"Gargantis wakes, Eerie quakes ..."*

"... and all falls into the sea," Violet finishes.

Mr Seegol forces a grin. "Ah, but you have come for chips, not old sayings and superstitions."

"Chips!" I cry, eager to get on to more important business. "Yes, please! Will this do, Mr Seegol?"

And I pull a silver napkin ring from my pocket and roll it across the table. Mr Seegol scoops up the ring and turns it around in the light.

"Victorian," I explain, nodding at the object in Seegol's hand. "Nice curly-wurlies on it. Only a bit dented. It was handed in at the Lost-and-Foundery a hundred years ago, so I signed it out for good just this morning. No one will be coming to collect it now, so it's mine, according to the rules. Good enough for chips, Mr Seegol? And maybe some of those crispy scampi sticks?"

Seegol rubs the napkin ring with his sleeve, making it gleam, and looks satisfied.

"You should let me pay one of these days," Vi says to me. "Now that I have a job of my own."

"Job?" Mr Seegol looks at Violet in surprise. "You have a job?"

"Violet lives at the book dispensary now," I explain, referring to Eerie-on-Sea's peculiar bookshop. "She's Jenny Hanniver's assistant, helping people consult the marvellous mechanical mermonkey. Helping it choose books for them, I mean."

"The mermonkey!" A faraway remembering sort of expression spreads over Seegol's face. "I haven't seen the mermonkey for so long."

"Then you should visit us sometime," says Violet, "and see what the mermonkey chooses for you."

"Ah, perhaps, perhaps..." The restaurant owner smiles a sad smile. Then he bows slightly and heads back to his kitchen to put chipped potato in the fryer.

"He won't ever come to the book dispensary, will he?" Violet whispers to me, watching him go.

I don't answer. Everyone knows that Mr Seegol never strays far from the pier.

"You should, though, Herbie," Violet says then. "When was *your* last time?"

"Me?" I reply. "But I visit you and Erwin in the bookshop all the time."

"I don't mean visit. I mean consult the mermonkey. When was the last time you asked it to choose a book for you, Herbert Lemon?"

My mouth falls open. It's a second or two before I remember to close it.

"Herbie?"

"I … I've already had a book from it," I say eventually. "Once. When I first arrived in Eerie-on-Sea. I don't need another one, thanks."

"But that was years ago!" Violet looks amazed. "Are you saying you've never thrown a coin in the mermonkey's hat since?"

I fold my arms and say nothing. The thing about the mermonkey is that it never gives you the book you want – oh, no, that would be too easy. And it won't choose the book you were expecting, either. No, it will be the book you *need*, or so Jenny Hanniver says. And that, you see, is my problem.

"What was it?" says Vi, as if reading my mind. "Come on, Herbie! It's obvious you didn't like the mermonkey's choice. So, what was the book?"

"I thought it was supposed to be private," I say at last. "The book you're dispensed."

"Well, not always. It depends. We've been getting a lot of fishermen in lately, since the storm blew up. Some of them haven't visited the mermonkey for years, so I help them."

"The fishermen?" I reply, happy to change the subject. "Since when do they bother with books?"

"Hey, everyone bothers with books." Violet gives me a stern look. "They just need to find the right one, that's all. Besides, the fishermen of Eerie have plenty of time on their hands right now. They can't go out to sea in this storm: the wind tears their sails to shreds, and the one motorboat that tried had its engine exploded by lightning. The fishermen are grounded."

"They'll be in the pub, more likely." I grin. "There won't be much reading done in there."

"It's not funny, Herbie," Violet replies. "One fisherman has drowned already. And now the townsfolk are starting to get scared, what with the stormquakes and everything."

"Stormquakes?"

"Come on, Herbie!" Violet cries. "Surely you've noticed. Even down in that cellar of yours. The storm is so fierce it makes the ground shake. Cracks have started to appear in Eerie Rock itself."

"But how can a storm do that?"

"Maybe you'll find the answer to that in a book." Violet smiles sweetly. "Like I said, you just need the *right* book, that's all."

And she raises one eyebrow at me.

"I'm not telling you, Violet!" I snap. "I got a bad book from the mermonkey. That's all. It must happen sometimes, and it happened to me. So I'll leave your mermonkey to the fishermen and the tourists, thanks very much. And that's the end of it."

"Herbie!"

But I won't be Herbied, not this time. I'm not sure even Jenny knows the title of the awful book I was dispensed when I first came to Eerie-on-Sea, and that's how it should stay.

It's a relief when our chips arrive.

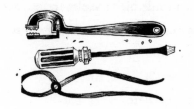

CAT IN A BOX

WE NOTICE SOMETHING'S WRONG as soon as we get back to the Lost-and-Foundery. Well, not exactly "as soon as" – it takes us a moment to shake the sting of the storm from our ears and get our breath back. But *then* we notice it.

"What's all this?" says Violet, picking something off the floor.

"Looks like slivers of wood," I reply, spotting more splinters scattered around on the threadbare rug.

"I'm pretty sure this mess wasn't here when we left." Vi picks up a few more slivers and splinters. "And all these bits of wool, too."

"Wool?"

"Yes." Vi holds her hand out to show me.

"And this looks like white fur…"

Her voice trails off as we stare at each other. Then we both swing around to look at the box of lost scarves by the fire.

"Erwin!"

The cat isn't there.

Violet runs to the box and rummages around the scarves, even though there's no way a big old moggy like Erwin could be hiding in there. He's gone.

"But he can't be," says Violet.

"Of course he can," I reply. "He could have crept up into the hotel, or maybe he's hiding somewhere else in the cellar."

"Then how did all this splintered wood and shredded wool get here?"

"Cats sometimes have crazy moments," I say. Although even as I say it, I know this isn't the answer. Erwin's not that kind of cat. I stoop and pick up another clump of white fur and peer at it through the magnifying glass.

"Oh, no…"

"What?" says Violet.

"This fur? The ends of it are neat. As if it has been snipped off."

"*Snipped?*"

Slowly we turn again, this time to look at the overturned bucket, the one we used to trap the strange clockwork hermit crab. It's where we left it, the heavy books still piled on top. But when we look around the back, we immediately see where all the splinters have come from. In the side of the bucket is a ragged hole, as if something small and determined has cut, drilled and sawn its way out. There's a mass of shredded wool there too – the remains of the old jumper.

Violet lifts the books and kicks the bucket over, spilling woollen scraps everywhere. But there's no sign of the little clockwork contraption.

"Do you think…?" Violet looks around, holding the heavy books as if she might need to use their squashing powers at any moment. "Do you think that that *thing* is hiding somewhere in the cellar too?"

I take my Lost-and-Founder's cap off the peg, put it on and manage not to wince when the elastic strap pings my ear.

"First," I say, "we need to check on Erwin. Look over there!"

I point towards the big wooden toolbox I got the winder keys out of earlier. There is more white fur on the floor here than anywhere else.

"Did you shut that box?" says Vi. "Herbie, I thought you left the toolbox open!"

"I did."

We hurry over to it, but when Violet reaches for the lid, she hesitates.

"What if when we open it...?" She turns to me. "What if poor Erwin is...?"

"What if he isn't, though?" I reply.

"Yes, but what if he *is*?" Violet wrings her hands. "If we don't look, then at least he might not be."

"Yeah, but right now he IS and ISN'T *at the same time*, and that's no good for a cat. Open the box, Vi!"

And that's when we hear a very loud, and very impatient, "Miaow!" from under the toolbox lid – the kind of miaow that sounds more like an annoyed human saying it than a cat miaowing it.

Violet flings the box open.

Erwin is sitting there, among the screwdrivers and pliers and oily rags, looking very uncomfortable and out of place. His deep coat of fur is missing tufts all over, as if someone tried to give him a haircut while he was running away. On one side of his nose his whiskers have been snipped short. His ears lie flat, and his eyes are full of thunderous indignation.

"Erwin!" Violet cries as she scoops him up.

They say cats can't smile, but as I watch Erwin being fussed over by Violet, his expression of outrage evaporates, his eyes close with happiness and he starts to rumble an enormous purr of relief and contentment.

"Oh, Erwin," Vi murmurs into his fur. "If only you could talk, you could tell us what happened..." Then she looks out at me and grins, because – well, because with Erwin things can get quite surprising. But one look at the cat, furiously rubbing his head on Vi's chin, tells me he's not in the mood for a chat right now.

"It's pretty obvious what happened anyway," says Violet. "Erwin was attacked by that clockwork shell. But could it really have cut through the bucket using only that tiny scissor claw?"

"Who's to say it has only that claw?" I reply. "There could be anything in that shell. It could be a walking Swiss army knife for all we know."

"I suppose you're going to say, 'I told you so'." Violet avoids my eye.

"No need. You've said it for me. But really, Vi, just because something *can* be wound up, or a button *can* be pressed, or a lever *can* be pulled, that doesn't mean it *should*."

"No wonder you never had any adventures till I came

to town," Vi declares, flopping with Erwin into my armchair. "With ideas like that!"

"I had adventures!" I reply. "Some really quite big ones, actually. And Erwin never got shaved in any of them. After all, the thirteenth rule of lost-and-foundering clearly states—"

"Wait!" says Vi. "What's that?"

"Don't interrupt and I'll tell you."

"No, I mean that sound." Vi waves me quiet. "Can you hear it? Listen!"

So I do. And I can.

Above the constant rumble of the gale outside, and the boom and crack of thunder, we can hear the murmur of voices raised in alarm. Voices up in the hotel lobby. And somewhere in it all, Mr Mollusc's peevish tones carry down to my cellar with the words "But ... but ... you can't bring *that* in here!"

"Something's happening," I say, and Violet raises her eyebrow.

"Yes. It is." She stands up and puts Erwin in the chair. "And what do we do when something happens?"

"Well, we take a look, but..."

"Then what are we waiting for?"

And so, together, we creep up the stairs to investigate.

A DISMAL BUSINESS

THE LIGHT IN MY CUBBYHOLE is off – the Lost-and-Foundery is closed, remember? – so it's easy for Violet and me to stay hidden in the shadows. We peer over the desk into the brightly lit lobby of the Grand Nautilus Hotel.

A group of dishevelled people are struggling through the great revolving doors, the storm still snatching at them as they enter. I see at once that they are local fishermen. They're grunting and gasping as they carry something between them, something tangled in an old fishing net. Mr Mollusc is wringing his hands and dancing from foot to foot as he protests.

"This is an outrage! We are a hotel, not a fishmonger's! Take this frightful object away before

I am forced to call the authorities!"

"This 'frightful object', as you call it," says a voice I know well, "isn't an object at all but a person. A person in need of urgent medical attention."

That's Dr Thalassi speaking – the town's medical doctor. He's also the curator at the Museum of Eerie and a distinguished member of the local community. Not that you'd guess that by looking at him now as he enters the hotel: his hair, usually so neat, has been storm-blasted in all directions, and his characteristic bow tie is wonky. The spectacles perched on his Roman nose are streaming with water, and there's a strand of seaweed over one bushy eyebrow.

"Bring her over here, into the light," he directs, and the fishermen heave their burden to the centre of the lobby. "Mr Mollusc, kindly make yourself useful and send to the kitchen for a large serrated knife."

And who is this person in urgent need of medical attention? Who is so hopelessly tangled in the old fishing net?

Well, at first I think it's another fisherman, mostly because of the wellington boots and waxed coat the figure is wearing. Also, the fishing net is surely a clue. But "her"? Almost all the fishermen in Eerie are, well, fisher*men*.

I rise up behind the desk slightly, to get a better look, and Violet does the same.

A kitchen boy, summoned by a snap of Mr Mollusc's fingers, hurries into the lobby with a big knife in a block of wood. The doctor takes it and begins carefully sawing through the net. There's a moment of hush as he works. Mr Mollusc, surrounded by a knot of hotel staff, stands to one side, while the group of grizzled fishermen loiter on the other, dripping and looking completely out of place in the lobby. Then the last rope is cut, and someone wearing many layers of coats, scarves and woolly jumpers rolls out onto the floor. On her head are at least three hats, tied on with a piece of string.

"Mrs Fossil!" Violet gasps.

And it's true. Eerie-on-Sea's one and only professional beachcomber is now lying in a pool of seawater and chopped rope on the hotel's marble floor.

"Wendy?" says Dr Thalassi, crouching beside her and feeling for a pulse in her neck. "Wendy Fossil, can you hear me?"

Mrs Fossil twitches, then coughs up a quantity of water and a few pieces of kelp. She nods in response to the doctor's repeated question, and a small smile spreads over her face.

"What's she got?" Violet whispers to me. "She seems to be holding something."

Sure enough, Mrs Fossil's arms are wrapped around a large object – an object that is itself wrapped in her tatty old waxed coat.

"Your patient lives, Doctor," says Mr Mollusc with a sniff. "All's well that ends well. Now, if you would kindly take this scruffy person home, I can get back to running a respectable hotel."

"Mrs Fossil, I need to examine you," says the doc, ignoring old Mollusc completely. "You nearly drowned. Please let go of that thing in your coat. What were you doing down on the beach in this storm anyway?"

"It's low tide," murmurs Mrs Fossil, weak and soggy from her ordeal. "Low tide after a storm ... best time for beachcombing..."

"But it's not *after* the storm, is it?" says the doctor, sitting her up. "The storm is worse than ever. You shouldn't have been anywhere near the sea in this weather."

"Aye." The fishermen nod in agreement as another crash of thunder makes the windows rattle.

"But, Doc," Mrs Fossil says. "If I hadn't been near the sea ... if I hadn't been down on the beach ... I wouldn't have found ... have found..."

"Found what?" Mr Mollusc demands, interested despite himself.

"I wouldn't have found –" Mrs Fossil's voice is no more than a whisper now – "the greatest beachcombing treasure of my whole life."

And with that she faints away. As she does, her arms fall to her sides, her coat slips open and something astonishing rolls out, coming to rest in the mass of cut-up net and seaweed on the hotel lobby floor.

It's a fish.

But not a living creature. This is a fish made from aqua-green glass – frosted over with age and the sea, but still recognizable from its fine workmanship as a very large, and very ancient-looking, fish-shaped bottle. It's about two Erwins long, and three quarters of an Erwin wide at its fattest, give or take a whisker. Its mouth, a perfect circle, is stoppered up by a solid-looking seaweedy mass. And as we stare, the bottle does something amazing.

It trembles.

All on its own it trembles, and there's a brief flicker of light from somewhere inside it.

"Fascinating!" says Dr Thalassi. "How extraordinary."

Predictably, it's Mr Mollusc who gets over the strange sight first.

"Humph. I don't see why. It's just a piece of old junk."

"Old junk!" Now it's the doctor's turn to be outraged. "Can't you see from the design how extremely old this bottle is? I wouldn't be surprised if it's a *thousand* years old. And besides, look!"

The doc points, but we're all looking at the bottle anyway, which is quivering and flickering with light again."

"Oh, that's … that's nothing," says Mr Mollusc, though he doesn't sound too sure. "It's just shaking with the storm. The whole hotel is shaking with the storm."

"It's like there's something inside," says one of the fishermen in wonder.

"Aye," says another. "Something inside, trying to get out."

"In that case, it definitely needs to be removed from the hotel," Mr Mollusc declares, noting with irritation that several more fishermen have drifted into the lobby to see what's going on. "Before some horrible, slimy glow-in-the-dark sea slug comes out and makes even more mess. We have our guests to think of."

"For once, I agree," says the doc. "It can't stay here. I will have it brought to the museum immediately…"

Mrs Fossil sits up.

"No," she splutters.

"Oh, forgive me," says Dr Thalassi. "I was forgetting my patient. Bringing this amazing find to the museum can wait till—"

"No!" Mrs F splutters again. "I won't let you take it, Doctor. I won't! *I* found it. It belongs to me, fair and square. I won't let you bully me into handing it over, no matter how *extraordinary* or *historical* you tell me it is. I'm keeping it, and that's that."

"But..." It's the doctor's turn to splutter. "But, my dear Wendy, surely you can see that this is no ordinary beachcombing knick-knack..."

"Knick-knack!" Mrs Fossil draws herself up straight and pulls the soggy hats from her head. "That's just like you to call my treasures 'knick-knacks'. My Flotsamporium is just as good as your fancy museum, and *all* the things I find have stories behind them, even the littlest sea-glass pebble or tide-rolled runcible spoon."

"But..."

"But nothing!" Mrs Fossil gets to her feet, her wellies squeaking on the polished floor. "I've been collecting messages in bottles on Eerie Beach since I was knee-high to a penguin, and I'm not about to let you snaffle such a fine and dandy one as this."

"This is not a message in a bottle," says the doc, standing himself and looming over the beachcomber. "If anything, this is a message *on* a bottle."

"What do you mean?"

"I mean, take a look on the side." He bends down and taps the glass bottle with his finger. "Can you see that? Have you any idea what that is?"

Everyone leans in to get a close look, though Vi and I have no chance of catching a glimpse of anything from this distance.

"It looks like ... writing?" Mrs Fossil blinks. "Funny writing, on the side of the bottle."

"Funny writing!" Dr Thalassi scoffs. "This is an inscription in Eerie Script. It is nothing less than the secret letters of the ancient fisherfolk of Eerie."

At these words, the fishermen gathered there visibly react and exchange expressions of surprise.

As if choosing this very moment, there is an almighty thunderclap over the hotel, and the ground beneath us trembles. Flakes of brick and plaster fall from the lobby ceiling, and one of the grand arched windows cracks from side to side.

"Gargantis wakes!" cries a fisherman.

"Eerie quakes!" cries another.

"Gargantis indeed!" Dr Thalassi turns his stern gaze on the fishermen, brushing plaster from his shoulder. "The storm might be bad, but there's no need for superstitious nonsense."

"That's easy for you to say, Doctor," growls a wiry old fisherman, stepping out from the rest. "But this is a Dismal business. You said so yourself."

"Eerie Script?" Mrs Fossil looks confused. "I've never heard of such a thing."

"Then by your own admission, the bottle cannot belong to you," says the wiry fisherman. "Eerie Script is the secret writing of Saint Dismal himself, The First Fisherman of Eerie-on-Sea. And so, by ancient law, this fish-shaped bottle belongs to us."

BLAZE

"AYE!" DECLARE THE FISHERMEN, forming a threatening crowd. "By the beard of Saint Dismal, this bottle is ours!"

Dr Thalassi raises his finger and protests, just as Mrs Fossil puts her hands on her hips and does the same. The atmosphere grows heated, and Mr Mollusc tries to break into the argument, telling everyone to leave. Near by, momentarily forgotten despite being the cause of all this trouble, the strange glass bottle quivers again and gives its eerie flicker.

I'm just beginning to think that some sort of riot is about to break out in the hotel, when I notice someone pushing his way to the front of the fishermen. He's a boy a few years older than me and Vi – tall and gangly and wearing oil-stained overalls that are too short in the leg. He's pale and freckled, with a flop of red hair over one eye. His eyes go wide when he sees the bottle, and he starts to speak, but his voice is drowned out by the older men.

So he does something unexpected.

He snatches the bottle up and holds it over his head.

"If this fish bottle should go to anyone," declares the boy in a cracked teenage voice, "it should go to my uncle Squint! He's ... he was..."

The boy falters as all eyes in the lobby swivel to look at him. His cheeks flare with embarrassment, as if they are trying to compete with his hair, and his arms begin to tremble.

"Careful!" Dr Thalassi and Mrs Fossil cry together.

The boy lowers the bottle back to the floor, and everyone breathes out in relief.

"Your uncle?" says the wiry old fisherman. "Old Squint Westerley?"

"Of course," the boy replies. "He knows more about Eerie Script than anyone."

Dr Thalassi looks offended at this, while the fishermen fidget and grumble to one another. When the wiry fisherman speaks again, his voice has an edge of threat in it.

"I'm not one to speak ill of the dead," he says, "and everyone already knows that Squint Westerley liked to poke his nose where no nose should be poked. But he's paid the ultimate price for his curiosity, lad, and left you all alone. You cannot claim the bottle for him now."

"But this bottle might give us answers!" the boy blurts out. "It might help us uncover the truth about Saint Dismal, and—"

"Truth!" The wiry fisherman looks aghast. "We don't need any 'truth' about Saint Dismal, bless his beard. We already have his *laws*. And those laws have served us well for centuries."

"But—"

"Enough!" the wiry fisherman bellows. "You cannot claim this bottle for a dead man, Blaze Westerley, no matter how much you miss him. And maybe if Squint had stuck to fishing instead of exploring and inventing and looking for answers to questions that don't need answering, he wouldn't have got himself drowned. No, this bottle is nothing but a bad omen, and if I had my way I'd throw it back in the sea."

"You will do no such thing!" cries Mrs Fossil. "I found it, and it will have pride of place in the window of my Flotsamporium— "

"As a precious historical artefact," Dr Thalassi interrupts, "this bottle belongs in my *museum*..."

And, with that, the argument seems set to erupt again.

But just then there's a loud, familiar *ting!* that reverberates around the lobby. Everyone turns to look in the direction of the beautiful old hotel elevator. The doors slide open with a *clack!* and golden light spills out. Silence falls, broken only by the rumble of the storm outside.

Then something emerges from the lift.

It's an antique-looking electric wheelchair made of bronze and wicker. Sitting in it is an even more antique-looking lady in a silk turban, tucked under a blanket embroidered with the crest of the hotel. Her face is wizened like that of an old tortoise, her mouth is surrounded by frothy white foam, and on her lap is a silver bowl with water sloshing in it. With one hand she guides the wheelchair forward with the use of a control box, and with the other she holds aloft a foamy toothbrush as if it's a sword she's just pulled from a stone.

"I was brushing my tooth," the lady says in a creaky old voice, "when I heard the commotion. Mr Mollusc, kindly explain to me what is happening in my hotel."

"Lady Kraken!" I whisper, clutching my cap.

"*That's* Lady Kraken?" Vi whispers back. "I'm not sure I've ever actually seen her."

And that's not surprising. Lady Kraken, the owner of the Grand Nautilus Hotel, lives in a vast suite of rooms on the top floor. She hardly ever leaves those rooms, and very few people in the town will have clapped eyes on her at all. Even I have seen her only a handful of times, and that was enough to last me for ever.

"Your Ladyship!" cries Mr Mollusc, raising his hands in a motion that seems to say, *Don't blame me!* and *I can explain!* all at once. "I ... I was just dealing with a little disagreement ... an indelicate unpleasantness ... a regrettable misunderstanding of a most peculiar kind ... a..."

"Stop wittering, man, and spit it out," snaps Lady Kraken. She looks around at the group of wild-haired fishermen, at Mrs Fossil in her many soggy layers, at the doc with his skew-whiff bow tie and at the hotel staff cowering behind Mr Mollusc. "Is it a revolution?"

"It is more in the nature of a beachcombing dispute." Mr Mollusc clasps his hands together. "An item of alleged significance has come to light ..."

"Has been *found*!" declares Mrs Fossil. "By me."

"… been found," Mollusc continues. "An item that the doctor thinks is of some value…"

"*Historic* value, that is, Lady Kraken." The doctor gives a respectful nod in the old lady's direction.

"Historic value, indeed." Mr Mollusc grins desperately at Dr Thalassi. "But the fishermen seem to feel strongly that the item is theirs by right…"

"And so it is!" declares the wiry old fisherman. "It is a Dismal business."

As if conjured by these words, the storm spews lightning and thunder once more, shaking the hotel to its foundations. Everyone looks skyward in alarm, while Mr Mollusc cowers before his employer.

"But I assure you, Your Ladyship, I have it all under control…"

Lady Kraken propels her electric wheelchair past the hapless hotel manager as if he isn't there, and she comes to a whirring halt beside the strange fish-shaped bottle.

"And this is it, is it?" she says. "The cause of all the hullabaloo?"

She unhooks an antique backscratcher from the side of her chair and gives the bottle a good sharp tap. The bottle shudders, and the eerie light flickers inside it once again.

"It is," says the red-haired boy. He approaches the old lady respectfully, clutching a skipper's cap in his hands. "My uncle would have known what to do with it."

"And where is this knowledgeable uncle now?"

"Lost," the boy says. "At sea."

Lady Kraken squints at him.

"And you think this bottle might be a clue to finding him again?"

The boy says nothing. But you can tell from his face that he does.

"And what is your name, young man?" Lady K asks.

"Blaze." The boy stares at the floor. "Blaze Westerley."

"Well, Mr Westerley, I have heard enough claims for now." The lady twirls her toothbrush. "Maybe I should just claim this fishy old bottle for myself. After all, it is in *my* hotel lobby."

There's a rumble of discontent at this, but no one – not even the fishermen – seems brave enough to argue with the venerable owner of the Grand Nautilus Hotel.

"But of course I won't," Lady Kraken continues, giving the bottle another tap. "I already know it doesn't belong to me. Deep down, everyone always knows whether or not something really belongs to them."

And she sweeps a wizened eye over everyone in the room.

"What we need right now," she continues, "is someone wise and true to decide on the rightful owner of this curious bottle."

"Couldn't you do that, Your Ladyship?" Mr Mollusc bows with an ingratiating smile. "I'm sure you could."

"No, I don't have time for all this." The lady waves the suggestion away. "Besides, I already have someone to handle such matters for me."

"You do?" says Dr Thalassi.

"Naturally," says Lady Kraken. "And he's been here all along, listening in on everything from his hiding place over there. Isn't that right, Herbert Lemon?"

And I freeze where I am, peering over the desk of my Lost-and-Foundery, as everyone in the lobby turns to look at me.

THE DUNDERBRAIN

SLOWLY, I STAND UP.

"Er, hello," I manage to say.

"Herbert Lemon!" snaps Mr Mollusc, clearly relieved to be back on safe ground shouting at me. "You will address Her Ladyship in the correct manner. Get out here, boy, and stop fiddling with your cap."

I look down at Violet, who is still crouching below my desk. She gives me a nod of encouragement. So I tug the front of my uniform straight, flip open the hinged part of the desk, and step out into the lobby as if everything's fine and I'm not at all being stared at by dozens of angry people.

"But," says Dr Thalassi, who is the first to recover from the surprise, "this bottle is ancient, Lady Kraken.

Its origins are lost in the mists of time. How can Herbie return such an artefact to its rightful owner? How can there even *be* a rightful owner, after all this time?"

"That is precisely why I should have it," says Mrs Fossil. "Whatever happened to 'Finders, keepers'?"

The fishermen begin to grumble.

"Enough!" Lady Kraken cries. "I have every faith in my Lost-and-Founder to discover the best solution to this problem. He is, after all, an expert. Come, Mr Lemon, come closer." And she beckons me with a claw-like hand.

I approach my employer and stand beside her wheelchair. She motions for me to lean in, her wrinkled head bobbing towards mine.

"Juicy conundrum, this, isn't it?" she says in a low voice only I can catch. "Think you're up to it?"

"Um…" I begin to say.

"Of course you are!" she cries, slapping me on the back. It feels like being hit with a sock full of dry twigs. "You don't want to be a dunderbrain all your life, do you, boy?"

"Well…" I venture, but the old lady silences me with a crooked finger.

"Just remember our deal," she whispers.

"Deal?"

"Yes, the deal! You said you would be my eyes and ears in the hotel, remember? You said you'd report any funny business to me. Well, something tells me funny business is afoot right now. I feel it, boy – feel it in my waters."

"Your waters?" I squeak, trying not to visualize this. "Right. Got it, Your Ladyness."

"Good lad!" Lady Kraken cackles. Then she speaks up so everyone can hear. "That's all sorted, then. And now, I will retire to my bedchamber. I haven't yet brushed my backside."

"Your ... your backside?"

"Yes," says the lady, swishing the toothbrush in the silver bowl before placing it in her mouth, "the backshide of my toosh. Goodnight!"

And with this she whirrs away to the elevator and trundles inside, the doors sliding shut behind her.

Everyone turns back to look at me.

I try a grin. Well, what else can I do?

There is a rule of lost-and-foundering – number eighteen, if you're wondering – that says: *When in doubt, brazen it out.* I've often wondered what it means, but as I stand there blinking under the frosty gaze of all the people in the lobby, I suddenly think I know exactly what that rule is all about. It means I can't stand here blinking any longer. It means I've got to do something, and fast.

"I need one of those," I say to a member of the hotel staff who is standing near by with a stack of freshly folded towels. "It's for important Lost-and-Founder business."

I drape a towel over the fish-shaped bottle, tuck it all around, and lift the whole thing into my arms before anyone can act or speak.

It's as I'm marching back to my cubbyhole, my arms full of bottle, that I happen to glance up the main lobby staircase and see something I wish I hadn't: Deep Hood, picked out in sudden lightning, watching us all.

I hurry down to my cellar as the thunder roars behind me.

"You were amazing!" says Violet.

We're at the foot of the stairs to my cellar, and I'm still clutching the ancient fish bottle wrapped in the white towel. Well, it *was* a white towel. Now it's already quite green and seawatery from the object inside. Up above, voices are raised in protest as Mr Mollusc clears the lobby and sends everyone home.

"I don't feel very amazing," I say, staggering into the cellar. "Help me get this thing safely down on the floor."

Between us we manage to lay the bottle out, bunching the towel around it like a nest. In the warm light of my Lost-and-Foundery, the bottle glows aqua-green and strange. I tap it gently with my foot. Immediately, it gives a little tremble, and the flickering light flashes inside.

"What's doing that?" says Vi, her face lit up with fascination and wonder. "It's almost as if there's something living inside it. But there can't be, can there?"

I shrug.

"It looks firmly stoppered to me," I say, peering at the bung in the end. "I don't think anything could get either in or out of that."

"What about the 'funny writing' as Mrs Fossil called it?" says Violet. "This must be it here."

And she points to a line of embossed symbols that run along one side of the bottle:

✝•ᚠᚱⱴᚠ•ᚢ•ᚾ⁝ᚢ∟ᛐᛕᚠⱽᛐᛕᚱᛁᛐᚼᛕᛐᚠ⁝Ⅹ

And then, on the other side:

✝ᚠ•ᚠᚱⱴᚾ•ᚢᛐ•ᛁⱴᚾᛕⱽ•ᛕⱽᛕᚱᛁⱴⱴᛁ•ᚠᛕⱽⅩ

"Look, there's more of it around the rim."

"Mrs F's not wrong," I reply. "It *is* funny. I wonder what it means."

Now it's Violet's turn to shrug.

"Looks like some kind of ancient runes," she says.

Erwin, who has been watching all this from behind my big armchair, cautiously approaches the bottle. He reaches out a hesitant paw and touches the glass. The bottle shakes and gives another flicker.

"Of course," says Vi, looking at me with a twinkle in her eye. "You know what I'm going to say now."

I quickly run through all the daring, crazy, unlikely and infuriating things Violet Parma could say right now, but I find it impossible to decide which one she's referring to.

"I'm going to say –" Vi grins – "that the only way to find out what's inside this bottle is to open it."

CALAMITOUS
WEATHER

"RIGHT," I SAY, grabbing the tip of my index finger to begin counting the reasons why we are NOT going to open this bottle. "Firstly, it's not ours to open. Secondly, we don't know if it's dangerous…"

"OK, OK." Violet sighs. "I get it. Still, I think deep down you know I'm right."

"Like you were right to wind up that shell thing?"

"But I think I *was* right to do that," says Vi. "We found out a lot about the clockwork shell by winding it up – and anyway, no harm was done."

Erwin clears his throat.

"Well, all right, *some* harm was done." Vi gives the cat a ruffle on the head. "But if we're not going to open the bottle, what are we going to do? And how on earth are you supposed to decide who gets to keep it?"

I say nothing. After all, Dr Thalassi is right – how can there ever be a rightful owner of something that looks as though it's been in the sea for centuries. I'm more used to signing things this old *out* of my Lost-and-Foundery – unclaimed, after a hundred years – than signing them in. I already think I should probably just give the bottle back to Mrs Fossil, on the quiet. And yet, it does look very old and historical…

"I'm going to do what I always do when a lost thing comes in," I say. "Look for clues. And I'd say the funny writing on the side of the bottle is the best clue we have."

"The Eerie Script," says Violet. "And what did the fishermen call it? A dreary business?"

"A Dismal business," I reply. "They mean it's got something to do with Saint Dismal."

But I can see from Violet's face that she needs more of an answer than that.

"Saint Dismal," I continue, "was the most famous fisherman of Eerie-on-Sea. At least, according to legend. He is said to have saved the town from disaster, so the fishermen think he's a hero. And he, er, he had a very long beard."

"Is that all you know about him?" says Vi. "*How* did he save the town, Herbie? What was the disaster? And what about the secret writing?"

I shrug. But then a light bulb goes on over my head.

"Wait, I probably *can* tell you more."

I go to my lost-books bookcase and start pulling out cardboard boxes. Eventually I find the right one and tip it out on the rug.

"What are all those?" says Vi.

"Guidebooks," I explain. "For Eerie-on-Sea. The summer tourists buy them but lose them all the time. I hardly ever get to return one, but I'm supposed to look after them, just the same."

I pick up a pamphlet with lots of pictures, and flick through it.

"Here," I say, handing it to Violet. "This is Saint Dismal."

On the page is a photo of the church in Eerie. It shows the statue of a wild-eyed old man dressed like a monk, holding a tall, crooked stick with a fish dangling on the end. He has an expression like thunder on his face, and a very long, scraggy beard that reaches to his feet.

"*Dismal,*" Violet reads from the caption. "*Patron Saint of Calamitous Weather, and First Fisherman of Eerie-on-Sea.*"

She taps the photo. "What's that sun thing over his head?"

Over the saint, where you'd normally expect a halo, the medieval sculptor carved a fiery star, which shoots zigzaggy rays down onto the holy man's bald patch.

"He always has that light over him, in all the pictures." I shrug. "It has a special name, too, the light, but I can't remember it."

"Once upon a time, a thousand years ago," Violet reads from the booklet, *"a fisher boy named Dismal sailed too close to Maw Rocks and was lost at sea. But his life was spared, and he returned days later with a strange and holy light over his head and the greatest catch of fish anyone had ever seen. The people called it a miracle and prepared a great feast of thanksgiving.*

"But soon there blew up from the ocean a storm so mighty that it threatened to destroy the town. The sky filled with fury, the ground shook and the people wept that Eerie Rock itself was falling into the sea. They named this storm 'Gargantis' and called it their doom. Only the boy Dismal resisted despair. Seeing that his home was threatened, he sailed fearlessly into the storm in his little coracle..."

"His little *what*-acle?" I jump in.

"His coracle," Violet repeats. "I think it's a type of boat. Anyway ... *he sailed fearlessly into the storm ... and*

using the strange and holy light, he lured Gargantis away and saved Eerie-on-Sea."

"Lured it?" I say, scratching under my cap. "How do you lure a storm?"

"You can't," says Violet. "It's just a story. Besides, look at this…"

And she holds up the guidebook to show what's on the next page. It's a very old drawing, of a kind Dr Thalassi calls a woodcut. And the woodcut shows something mind-boggling.

A vast creature – with the head of an anglerfish and dozens of fins along its sinewy body – is "swimming" in the sky over Eerie-on-Sea. It has two huge flippers, a low-slung mouth filled with tusks, and gigantic ichthyosaur eyes. The creature is wreathed in storm clouds and lightning that seem to pour off its fins. It uses its giant flippers to smash the town to pieces, while lots of little medieval people run away screaming.

"Yikes!" I say.

"Early depictions of Gargantis often portrayed it as an actual monster," says Violet, reading the caption under the drawing, *"to symbolize the monstrous nature of the storm.* Herbie, imagine a storm so powerful that it has its own name!"

There's another *KA-BLAM* of thunder and a fall of

brick dust from my cellar roof. The Lost-and-Foundery quivers as if the very foundations of the hotel are shifting.

"We don't have to imagine it!" is all I can say.

"After saving the town, Saint Dismal lived out the rest of his long days on a rocky island in Eerie Bay," Violet reads the last bit from the guidebook, *"protecting the town, and warning sailors and fishermen to keep away from Maw Rocks. He was famous for his bountiful catches and is considered the First Fisherman of Eerie-on-Sea. He is always depicted with the miraculous light over his head, known as the Gargantic Light."*

"That's it!" I cry. "I knew it had a special name! The Gargantic Light."

There's another boom of thunder outside, making my iron wood burner rattle.

"Gargantis wakes, Eerie quakes..." Violet says, repeating the old saying from Seegol's Diner as she closes the guidebook. "And all falls into the sea!"

"Not the hotel," I reply firmly. "The Grand Nautilus Hotel is built like a castle. My cellar must be the strongest place in the whole town."

But even I can hear the doubt in my voice as I say this.

"Anyway –" Vi throws the guidebook back in the box – "it's a strange legend, but there's nothing here about any secret writing. There is another clue we could try, though. That red-headed boy, Blaze Westerley. Do you know anything about him?"

"I've seen him around. He and his uncle are fishermen. They have a boat down in the harbour."

"Have you ever been on it?"

I blink at her.

"On what? Their *boat*? Of course I haven't!"

"You don't need to sound so surprised, Herbie. It's a seaside town, I just thought maybe..."

"Well, you thought wrong, then. These fishermen are hard, serious men. They don't take *passengers*. Besides, I never go on boat trips, Vi. Just in case."

"Just in case what?"

But I don't want to answer that.

Violet knows how I came to Eerie – washed up on the beach, barely conscious, in a crate of lemons. Even if I can't remember anything before that, it doesn't take a genius to guess I was in some sort of disaster at sea. So these feet are staying firmly on land from now on, thank you very much, and Violet should be able to figure this out for herself. But when I glance up, I see from Violet's face that she probably already has.

"Why won't you tell me what book the mermonkey chose for you, Herbie?" she asks. "When you first came to Eerie-on-Sea? You know which one it chose for me."

And that's true enough. I was right there when Violet was dispensed the book that led her to unravel part of the mystery of her parents' disappearance. And while she didn't exactly find them, she was at least left with the belief they are still out there somewhere, looking for her. It gives her hope that she will be reunited with them some day. But if Violet knew what book the mermonkey chose for me, she'd see right away that I have no such hope.

"I'll never tell you," I say, like I mean it, which I do. And I fold my arms for good measure. "No one in the world knows the title of my book, Violet, and that's the way it'll stay."

"Prr-up?" says a feline voice, and Erwin jumps into my lap. He stands there, his nose pressed up against mine, his tail waving with irritation.

And I suddenly remember that someone else *does* know the title of my book after all. Someone who is good at noticing things, without being noticed himself. And that someone also knows where I hid it.

"You wouldn't…!" I say to the cat.

But Erwin has already jumped off my lap and is walking purposefully towards my bookcase.

THE COLD, DARK
BOTTOM OF THE SEA

MAYBE IT'S BECAUSE I'm so good at caring for other people's stuff that I'm so bad at concealing my own. But honestly, you'd think I'd be on safe ground hiding a book I don't want anyone to know about on a bookcase crammed with lost books. After all, why would anyone know one of those books was special to me if they weren't told? Which is why it's so annoying that despite my best flying tackle, I can't reach Erwin before he gets to the bottom-most shelf on my bookcase and claws a slim black volume out from the rest.

Of course, Violet's there in a moment, grabbing the book and holding it up in triumph.

"Pesky cat!" I get to my feet and chase the little beast a bit. I don't really want to catch him, but I do want him to know how cross I am. He jumps up onto the window ledge and hisses down at me.

I turn back to Violet.

"That's not fair!"

But Violet doesn't reply. She stares at the book in her hands and slumps back into my armchair. On her face is a look of horror.

I give a sigh and I plonk myself beside her. Now we're both looking at the cracked white title letters of the novel the mermonkey chose for me when I first came to Eerie:

The
COLD, DARK
BOTTOM
of the
SEA

Above the title is a white line across the cover that represents the surface of the water. On this line floats an iceberg, and beside it is the silhouette of a glittering luxury ocean liner, tipped back dramatically and sinking. Then, below the line and all around the title, tiny figures of men and women and children writhe and twist as they sink down, down, down to the depths. Across the lower edge of the black leather cover wave the white tentacles, feelers and claws of the abyssal horrors that lurk at the cold, dark bottom of the sea.

You don't need to read this book to know what it's about.

But I can already guess that the disturbing artwork isn't the only thing that's making Violet stare. Just below the title is the name of the author:

SEBASTIAN EELS

Of course, you've probably heard of Sebastian Eels. He is – or rather, he *was* – the most famous author who has ever lived in Eerie-on-Sea. He also turned out to be a grade A villain, who met his end in our last big adventure. And a monstrous end it was, too. He was the mortal enemy of Violet's father – and the main reason she has been left without parents at all. He can't hurt her now, but that doesn't mean he doesn't cast a long shadow over her life.

"I had no idea that bully had a link to you, too," says Violet, looking up at me.

I shrug.

"I've done my best to forget it. Besides, I don't think that's the reason the mermonkey chose this book for me."

And I point to the drowning people sinking to their doom on the cover.

"Herbie." Violet looks me straight in the eye. "When people consult the mermonkey, they search for meaning in the book it chooses for them. But the meaning they find depends on them." She lifts my book in the air. "This book doesn't have to mean—"

"It does," I interrupt with a sad nod. "I'm a castaway, a survivor. There's no need for me to wonder what happened to my parents, is there? Or my whole family, maybe. It's pretty clear what the mermonkey was trying to tell me. We were on a ship, and that ship sank."

"Herbie, have you actually read the book? Maybe, in the story, there's something else…"

"There isn't," I reply. "This book is the story of the SS *Fabulous* – a luxury liner that sank in the ocean. There's only one survivor mentioned in *The Cold, Dark Bottom of the Sea*, and he spends the rest of his life convinced he is destined to share the same fate as his shipmates. He never gets on a boat again, and neither will I. I know this book is only a novel, Vi, and not about real events, but the mermonkey gave it to me as a warning."

Violet looks shocked, and desperate to say something else. But in the end she just shakes her head.

"And I won't be getting any more books from the mermonkey, either," I add, glaring up at Erwin on his windowsill. He narrows his eyes at me.

Upstairs in the hotel, we hear the hour of 11 p.m. chime as the storm roars fiercer than ever. The last log in my little wood burner settles, and I decide not to throw in another. The strange antique bottle has gone quiet, as it lies – mysterious and enticing – in its pile of soggy towel in the middle of the floor.

"You can sleep here tonight, Vi," I say with a yawn. "And Erwin. Then we can make a proper start on The Case of the Fish-Shaped Bottle in the morning. In the meantime, *this* is going right out of sight."

And I pick up *The Cold, Dark Bottom of the Sea* by Sebastian Eels, bury it in the box of lost guidebooks, and shove the whole thing back on my bookcase.

"Maybe you're right," Violet agrees, looking more subdued than I've seen her for ages. "We need to get on with the next adventure, not worry over the remains of the last."

And with this she walks around behind the clothes rack to find her favourite spot, deep among the coats and lost blankets.

"Goodnight, Herbie."

Erwin jumps down from the window and follows her.

But I'm not in the mood for bed, not just yet. I turn down the lamp and settle back in my chair with a blanket. It feels strange now that someone else has seen my secret book, but it doesn't really change anything. I still want to forget all about it.

Outside, the storm thunders on, and my mind fills with bearded saints and ancient scripts and our strange new guest with his face lost in the shadow of a deep hood. Nameless, sightless creatures crawl into my imagination from the cold, dark bottom of the sea. It will be a miracle if I get any sleep tonight.

But sleep does come.

Only to be interrupted in the most extraordinary way imaginable.

TOUCHÉ!

AT FIRST, I DON'T KNOW what it is that wakes me. I open my eyes to see everything around me bathed in a cold blue as the small light of early morning creeps through my window. I have a vague sense that I heard something. *Did* I hear something?

Then I hear it again.

Ting.

It's a very small sound, as if something metal was lightly tapping against something glass.

Ting tang.

Quietly, I sit up.

In the gloom I see that there's something on the floor of my cellar, something that isn't usually there. Then I remember – it's the ancient bottle. My mind begins to turn around the question of where I can store this old bottle while I have it, since it can hardly live in the middle of the floor like that. I feel myself start to drift off to sleep again...

Ting tang tingle-CLANK!

I sit up again. My mouth falls open in disbelief – disbelief because the bottle is moving. Yes, *moving*! It has risen jerkily off the ground and is dipping one way then the other as it makes its way towards the stairs, to the sound of light tapping from little metallic feet.

I reach over to the table beside my chair, and my fingers feel around among the objects there. Magnifying glass? No. Screwdriver? No. Torch? Yes!

I point the torch and switch it on.

In the sudden beam of light, I see what is holding the bottle up.

It's the clockwork hermit crab!

Four long brass appendages are extended from the trumpet end of the shell and wrapped awkwardly around the bottle. Another four brass limbs reach to the ground, acting as legs. The whole thing is straining and stumbling under the bulk of the bottle as it reaches the first step. I sit there, struggling to take in what I'm seeing, as the shell makes an enormous effort and succeeds in climbing onto the first step, still balancing the bottle above it. Then it begins to climb to the next…

"No!" I shout, leaping from my chair and dropping the torch. I race across the cellar and grab the bottle.

There's a brief tug of war before the bottle slips free of the metal appendages, and I fall backwards, landing on my bum. The bottle escapes my hands and rolls away across the floor.

I scramble to my feet and switch on the main cellar light. I need to catch this stupid shell thing once and for all.

But the shell isn't trying to escape. It has righted itself and is standing at the bottom of the stairs on its four brass legs, the other four appendages raised towards me like the forelegs of a praying mantis. As I watch, fascinated and horrified all at once, there's a sudden *sschl-i-i-ik!* sound as steel blades slide out from each of the four raised arms.

Then, whirring with clockwork determination, the shell advances towards me.

In the log basket beside my wood burner is a poker. I grab it, my mind racing. I try to remember if there's a rule of lost-and-foundering that says it's OK to smash a lost object to smithereens if it tries to pinch your stuff and then attacks you with swords. I don't think there is one.

Too bad.

It's a shame to break such a remarkable thing, but it would be a greater shame to let it break me. And what if it went after Violet while she slept?

I lunge forward and swing the poker – which is heavy and made of iron – down onto the shell with all my might.

The shell parries my blow.

Three of its blade arms cross, and it catches the poker, absorbing the impact. I feel the poker being tugged from my grip as the mechanical shell twists its blades and attempts to disarm me.

I leap back and twirl the poker. Then I swing again, and again and again. The shell dodges from side to side, parrying my blows with sparks and stabbing forward with at least one blade each time. There's a sudden flash of pain, and I stumble backwards and look at my hand. There's a thin line of blood running down the back of it.

My mind spins. A few minutes ago I was sleeping soundly. Now I'm wide awake, sword-fighting a clockwork hermit crab. And the hermit crab is winning!

I fling the poker at it.

The hermit crab is caught by surprise and knocked off its feet. I don't wait for it to recover. Thanking my lucky stars I didn't take my shoes off last night, I run to the stricken shell – which is scrabbling to get up on its metal legs – and give the blasted thing an almighty kick up the trumpet.

The shell flies away from me, spinning out of control, and vanishes from view up the stairs. I hear a satisfying *pang!* as it hits the stone steps, and know with certainty that something has broken. I snatch up the poker and run to finish it off, but I see the legs of the hermit crab vanish over the desk in my cubbyhole above. There's the sound of little brass feet skittering away across the polished marble floor of the hotel lobby, then silence. The clockwork hermit crab has escaped once again.

I slump down on the stairs, halfway up.

Down below, in the cellar, I see a sleepy Violet appear. Beside her is an even sleepier Erwin.

"What's going on, Herbie?"

I'm about to answer when I notice something on the step beside me. It's a hinged rod of brass. I pick it up and turn it in the light. It's one of the sword arms of the hermit crab, broken off at a hinge and slightly bent. The steel blade is still extended and feels razor-sharp.

"What's going on," I say to Vi, "is that someone just tried to steal the bottle."

I show her the back of my hand, which is still bleeding slightly.

"And now Erwin's not the only one to have had a close shave with that little clockwork monster."

GENIE

WE PICK UP THE BOTTLE, and I'm relieved to see that there's no damage to it, not even a crack. As we lift it back into the nest of soggy towel in the middle of the cellar floor – I still haven't worked out where else to put it – we feel it tremble and see the light flicker inside.

"You think someone's controlling the clockwork shell?" says Vi, after I've explained what happened. "Or do you mean the shell is acting on its own and wants the bottle for itself?"

"I don't see how a clockwork hermit crab, no matter how complex, can want things for itself," I reply. "But is it really possible to control a thing like that remotely? I don't know."

I go to my repair desk, push some clutter aside and

place the severed brass arm in the light of the desk lamp.

"It's nicely made, this thing," I say, sitting and peering at the bent and broken limb through the magnifying glass. "And it looks old. I hate that I had to break it."

"Never mind about that, Herbie," says Vi. "You should get your hand cleaned up."

"Yeah, in a sec," I reply.

I take two pairs of rubber-jawed pliers and manage with a grunt to straighten the brass arm. This allows me, with a bit of careful fiddling, to get the blade to retract and the spring to reset. Now it looks as good as new. Well, except for the part that snapped.

"This arm only broke off because a small brass bolt sheered in two," I explain to Vi, who I can hear building up the fire in the stove behind me. "I'm sure I've got a spare part to fit that. I could probably get the hermit crab fixed up, if only I could catch the pesky thing and stop it from trying to chop us."

"I'm sure you could," says Violet. "But don't you think it's more important to figure out *why* it tried to take the bottle?"

"Maybe." I rummage in a little drawer full of bolts and screws. "If we can figure out the *why*, then that should lead us to the *who*… Ah, this should do it."

And I place a small nut and bolt neatly on my desk, beside the restored arm. It's made of steel, the bolt, and is a bit plain beside the beautiful workmanship of the brass limb, but it should fit nicely and make the thing work as good as new. And you never know – that shell might get handed in again one day, once its spring has wound down, and I could fix it.

"If someone is using the shell to try to steal the fish-shaped bottle," says Vi, "then that makes five, that we know of."

"Five what?"

"Five people who want the bottle: Mrs Fossil, Dr Thalassi, the fishermen as a group, the boy Blaze Westerley, and now some mystery person with a clockwork sidekick."

"That mystery person," I say, rinsing my hand in the sink and wrapping a cleanish sock around it, "must be the strange new guest who arrived in the hotel last night. The one who handed in the shell."

"What's his name?"

I shrug. "I just think of him as Deep Hood."

"He arrived *before* the bottle was found, though," Vi says. "Can he really count as someone who is claiming it?"

"Only just before," I reply, hearing the first gurgle of hunger from my stomach. "Maybe he knew the bottle had been found and was likely to be handed in. Anyway, if we're going to Scooby-Doo that list of names in order of suspiciousness, I reckon Deep Hood goes at the top."

There's a rattling sound and we both turn to look at the fish-shaped bottle. It quivers all by itself as light flickers somewhere in its frosty blue-green depths.

"And *I* reckon," says Violet, "that the very best way to Scooby-Doo this whole eerie mystery is to open that bottle right now and see what's inside."

A moment or two later, Vi and I are crouching down next to the bottle, our noses almost touching its cold, frosted exterior. At this close range, the detail of the fish's scales and fins is impressive. But, try as we might, we just cannot see *through* the glass.

"It's too foggy," I say. "Too, too ... sea-glassy? Is that a word?"

Violet doesn't answer but presses her ear against the glass. She gives the bottle a ringing tap with her fingernail, and it shudders and flickers with light in response.

"OK," I say with a sigh. "Maybe there's a way we could just *peek* inside. Without opening it completely, I mean."

"Peeking inside might not be enough, Herbie," Violet replies. Then she sees my face. "But I suppose it's better than nothing."

We crawl around to look at the stoppered end. Straightaway we see that getting that peek is going to be easier said than done.

"It stinks," says Vi, wrinkling her nose at the stopper, "like the bottom of the sea."

And it's true. The bottle appears to be stoppered with a plug of rubbery wax. Into this, generations of seaweeds have rooted, grown, died and then grown back again, hanging from the mouth of the bottle. The overall effect is that the glass fish looks as if it's throwing up some particularly nasty sushi.

"We could melt a small hole through it," I say. "If this really is wax, that is."

"Melt it how?"

"Well, by heating up the end of a screwdriver," I reply. "That way we could peek inside and then melt the hole closed afterwards. No one would ever know we'd done it."

Violet stares at me thoughtfully.

Then she snatches up a screwdriver from my repair desk and wedges it in the door of my wood burner – which is just starting to heat up nicely.

"I see," I say. "So that's decided, then? We're actually doing this?"

"Come on, Herbie, you want to know what's in there as much as I do." Violet shoves her hair out of her face. "And you said it yourself: no one will ever know we looked."

"And the thing inside?" I say. "What if it tries to come out?"

"The hole will be *tiny*," says Vi. "How could it come out?"

"It didn't matter how much or how little Aladdin rubbed the lamp," comes a voice from behind us, "the genie only came out because he wanted to."

We both turn. Sitting on my big tatty armchair, Erwin is watching us closely with his ice-blue eyes. Violet beams back at him. She loves it when he talks, though no one can ever predict when he will, or why he does. Like many of the eeriest things in Eerie-on-Sea, Erwin follows no rules that I know of.

"It's OK, puss," Violet says. "We'll be careful."

Erwin twitches the trimmed side of his whiskers, as though he's trying to tell us something. Then he licks his paw as if he's just like any other cat in the world.

And now the screwdriver is hot enough.

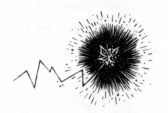

SPRIGHTNING

I PLACE THE TIP of the screwdriver against the wax, and it hisses. A curl of smoke rises and fills the cellar with a heady perfume. I expected it to smell foul, the melted wax, but instead it's strange – balanced somewhere between "!" and "?". It makes my nose tingle and my mind think of years ago, and faraway, and the sea.

With an effort, I push the hot screwdriver right through the wax stopper. After waiting a moment for the screwdriver to cool, I turn it by the handle and ease it back out. And now there's a neat little hole, narrower than a pencil, in the ancient wax.

I crouch down to look into it.

"What can you see?" Violet's voice is an excited whisper. "Herbie!"

I squint as hard as I can.

"I can't really see anythi—" I begin, but there's a flash, and something hot and fierce hits me on the nose.

"Ow!" I jump back, startled.

On the floor in front of me is a tiny flickering ember, singeing the rug.

"What did you see, Herbie?" says Vi, looking back at the bottle. *"What's in there?"*

"I don't think there's anything in there, Vi. At least, not now. I think what was in there was *that*."

And I point at the smouldering ember, which is starting to roll … no, *crawl* forward, as if on little hands and knees.

"What *is* it?" Violet crouches down beside me. "A spark?"

I reach down with one finger and give the tiny thing a poke.

It erupts with light.

Violet and I shrink back as the object – brilliant and fizzing now, like a blazing star – rises from the rug and darts at us, crackling with power.

Erwin gives a hiss of alarm and jumps from the chair. The fizzing light, as if spotting the terrified cat, darts towards him. Erwin runs to the window and scrabbles at it, but it's locked. The light swoops to a sparkling halt above him, and then it fires a miniature bolt of lightning down at the hapless feline. Erwin shrieks "YE-OW!" and leaps into the air, then flies in desperation towards Violet, the tip of his tail smoking.

In a moment we're on our feet, backing away.

"So much for just taking a peek!" I cry. "How are we going to get *that* back inside the bottle?"

The light approaches, spitting sparks in all directions. It makes another dive for Erwin, but Violet grabs the cat up in her arms. The light darts away but then swoops back to crackle angrily right in front of Violet's face.

"Now, just you keep back," Violet declares, wagging her finger at the light. "I'm not so easy to shock."

The light retreats a little, but then it surges forward again, spitting sparks into Violet's hair.

"Get away!" she shouts, swatting with her free hand and retreating into a corner.

"Hey!" I yell, grabbing up the fish-shaped bottle and holding the stopper end towards the light. "Over here! Get back in your bottle!"

The light flutters around to face me. There's a flash and a boom as it emits another miniature bolt of lightning. An old teddy bear in my lost-toys box explodes in a puff of stuffing and smoke, right beside my head.

I let out a squeak, and the bottle slips from my hands, dropping to the floor and rolling away.

And now the light is advancing towards me, brighter than ever, like a tiny wronged sun, burning to have its revenge.

"Can't we talk about this?" I gasp as I step back, trip over some lost shoes and fall into a basket of brollies. "I'm too young to fry!"

The light blazes as it closes in.

Then it sputters.

There's a flicker and a crackle, and the light fades.

The thing falls from the air, a tiny ember once again, and bounces on the rug.

And lies still.

Cautiously, I crawl towards it.

"Careful, Herbie!" Violet calls from across the cellar.

"It's OK," I say, though there's no way I can know that for sure, is there? "I think … I think maybe it's worn itself out. Whatever *it* is."

I lean forward and try to get a better look at the strange thing that escaped from the bottle. Now that it isn't blazing with fierce light, I see that it's actually a tiny figure, ember-bright, crouching on the floor as if exhausted. I watch, amazed, as two electrical arcs flicker out from the figure's back, forming shapes that look for all the world like wings. These arcs flutter for a moment, as if trying to fly, but then wink out again.

"It's OK," I say again, though this time in a softer voice and not to Violet. "I'm not going to hurt you. I'm … I'm Herbie. I'm the one who let you out of the bottle."

Down on the rug, a tiny pixie face stares up into mine.

"You don't want to go back in that bottle, do you?" I say. Then I add, because I suddenly know it's true, "I think you've waited a long, long time to be let out."

There's a brief electrical crackle that feels a lot like an answer to me. Then the little thing falls over, and its light goes out completely.

So I pick it up.

This probably seems like a brave thing to do, but really, I don't even think about it. I know a lost soul when I see one.

"Is it hot?" Violet whispers, coming to join me. "Does it burn?"

"No," I reply, cradling the tiny fairy figure in my cupped hands.

"It's amazing!" Violet's eyes are as big as scallop shells. "What do you think it is?"

Before I can answer, there's a tingling in my hands. The little figure starts to glow again.

"Herbie?"

"It's fine," I say. "I think. It's just … warm. A nice, cheering warmth. Like the little thing's getting strength from me and is grateful."

The light brightens, and soon it spills from my hands to gently bathe our faces. The pixie sits up, gazes up at me again and smiles!

"Hello," I say, grinning back, because I can't help it. "Feeling better?"

There's a crackle of light, and the tiny electrical wings reappear, this time beating with a strong, fizzing flutter. The figure vanishes from view as the light intensifies. Then it rises from my hands and flutters here and there before coming to settle just over my head.

Carefully, I get to my feet. The light remains just above my head. I take a step to the right, and the light follows. I step left, and the light moves left too. Something tells me it's here to stay.

"Wait!" Violet cries, pointing at our miraculous little guest. "Over your head like that, it looks like … could that be…?"

I turn and stare in a mirror. I see myself standing in

my crumpled Lost-and-Founder's uniform, an expression of amazement on my face as a crackling point of light hovers just above my head, showering me with tiny sparks.

"Bladderwracks!" I whisper.

"Just like on the statue of Saint Dismal," says Vi. "In the photo."

We look at each other.

"The Gargantic Light!"

HOODWINKS

"SHE SEEMS TO LIKE YOU," Violet says, and grins.

"She?"

"Well, she seems like a she to me," says Violet. "With all the lightning."

"Either way, at least she's not zapping things right now," I reply, opening my cellar window and pointing outside.

"OK, you can go," I say to the light over my head.

The light crackles some more and then plops down into my hair.

"Oi!" I cry. "Didn't you hear me? You're free."

But the tiny electrical fairy shows no intention of going anywhere. I look again at the mirror and see light streaming from my head as the little thing settles down deep in my scrappy blond locks.

"I can't go around with this over my head," I say to Violet. "People will notice. Mr Mollusc will use me as a standard lamp!"

"Try this." Violet hands me my cap.

Very carefully I lower the cap onto my head, trapping the light beneath it. Then I start working the elastic strap around my chin with only a minimum of pings. I take a step to the left, and then two steps back. The light remains where it is, hidden beneath the roya-porpoise-blue-and-gold trim of my official Lost-and-Founder's cap.

"There!" says Violet. "How does that feel?"

"Strange," I reply. "And a bit fizzy."

From up above, we hear the sounds of the hotel beginning to wake up: the clatter of suitcases, the murmur of voices and the tinkle of breakfast cutlery in the dining room.

"There's a plate of stale pastries up there with my name on it," I say to Vi as I straighten my uniform front. "I'm going to test out just how well hidden this light thing is by going up and getting our breakfast. Then we can work out what on earth to do about it."

With that, I climb up the stairs to my cubbyhole.

"Good morning, Herbie," says Amber Griss, the hotel receptionist, as I slowly cross the lobby towards the kitchen. "Why are you walking in that funny way? It's almost as if you have something hidden under your hat."

My scalp starts tingling.

I do a grin.

"Morning, Amber. Nothing hidden under my hat. Nothing at all."

"Well, just be sure to keep your head down today." Amber leans towards me and lowers her voice. "Mr Mollusc is still fuming about what happened last night. And he blames everything on you."

"Me!"

"I'm afraid so. He's not happy about that bottle being here, not happy at all, and he seems determined to make you pay for it. If I were you, I wouldn't do anything to draw attention to myself today."

There's a small explosion, and I feel the elastic stretch as my cap is lifted for a moment with the force of a miniature blast of lightning. I shout, "YOWZERS!" and then clap my hand over my mouth as smoke and the unmistakable pong of singed hair drifts out from under my cap.

"OK!" I say to Amber, who is now staring at me in

amazement. "Nothing to draw attention to myself. Got it. *Thanks!*"

Then I run.

I find my plate of leftover pastries in the kitchen, and I leave by the back passage without having any more exploding-cap incidents. But then I hear something that brings me to a skidding halt: the brisk, busybody footsteps of Mr Mollusc.

I duck into a shadow as the hotel manager turns a corner in the company of someone.

"I have already told you, sir," I hear him say in a panicky voice. "I asked Her Ladyship, and she refused to see you…"

The man beside Mr Mollusc swings around, blocking the manager's way. Even though he has his back to me, I recognize him as the tall stranger in the overlong coat and deep hood, the one who left the shell on my counter.

The stranger leans forward menacingly and murmurs something to Mollusc, something I can't hear.

"But … but…" I hear the manager protest. "I can hardly do that…"

Then Deep Hood raises his hands, takes hold of his hood and begins to pull it back. From my hiding place all I can see are the hotel manager's eyes bulging from his head. He goes so white he's almost see-through, as he shrinks back at the sight of whatever is revealed in the shadows of the hood.

"I'll do it!" he cries. "I'll ask her again!"

Satisfied, the stranger lets the hood fall over his features once more. He turns back in my direction.

I hastily reverse back into the kitchen, then run around to the hotel lobby the other way, pastries bouncing on my plate. I don't stop bouncing till I reach my Lost-and-Foundery.

It's half an hour later, and Violet and I have wiped the breakfast crumbs from our chins and pulled on coats and scarves.

"Are you bringing that, too?" I say as I watch Violet fold a large sheet of paper and slip it into her pocket with a pen.

While I was upstairs, Violet used a crayon to make a rubbing of the strange writing on the sides of the bottle.

"It's a clue, isn't it?" she replies. "Even if we can't read it."

Then we climb out through the window and find

ourselves blinking in the winter sun.

Eerie-on-Sea is battered and broken. The cobbles are strewn with smashed roof tiles, drifts of beach pebbles and splintered bits of boat that have been flung up by the storm tide. Windows are smashed, chimney stacks have collapsed, and all around, townspeople are sweeping and nailing and doing their best to make things right. Gusts still whip and snatch at our clothes, but the sky above has been wind-blasted free of cloud, and is filled with the pterodactyl cry of seagulls.

The storm isn't over, but it has moved on. It can still be seen out on the horizon – a vast mountain range of flickering cloud and angry shadow, rumbling across the bay. Twice before it has retreated like this, and twice it has returned, stronger than ever. Looking at it now, it's easy to imagine that it will be over the town again soon.

"Look at that!" Violet gasps, pointing to the cliffs. A section has collapsed, and there's a scar running along them, as if something gargantuan has gouged into the rock.

"Er..." I squeak. "Never mind that – look at *that*!" And I point behind us.

Across the side of the hotel, and rising up one of the towers, is another gouge mark – four jagged lines in the shattered brickwork. It looks for all the world as if a giant claw has raked the wall of the Grand Nautilus Hotel.

"Did lightning do that?" Vi asks. "That's one terrific storm!"

"I'm not sure 'terrific' is the word I would use," says a man sweeping broken glass near by. "Even the sea wall is cracked."

Sure enough, a fissure has appeared in the mighty stone wall and spread across the ground, creating a step in the promenade where there didn't used to be one.

"Gargantis wakes, Eerie quakes," Vi replies, quoting the old saying. It draws a sharp look from the sweeping man.

"A bit less of that talk, if you don't mind," he snaps. "If we get another pasting like last night, Eerie Rock really could fall into the sea – and take the whole town with it."

"You actually think that might happen?" I ask, feeling a twinge of anxiety in my scalp.

But the man just tuts at me and heads off, sweeping his heap of ruin away with him.

"I told you people are scared," says Violet. "Come on, let's find Blaze Westerley and get some answers."

So we make our way along the chaotic promenade towards the harbour, while Erwin leaps along the sea wall beside us. On our left loom the half-timbered gables of the Whelk & Walrus Pub, leaning more crazily than ever, its grubby sign creaking in the wind. Outside the pub, a number of fishermen are struggling with a rowing boat that has been lifted by the storm and deposited on the promenade. They sing one of their famous shanties as they work, but they stop what they're doing to glare sea-hardened stares at me as we pass.

"Good morning," says Violet brightly. "Rough night!"

The fishermen respond with a discouraging silence.

"It's good that the storm's gone," Violet tries again. "What's the weather forecast like?"

"Dismal," a fisherman replies grudgingly. "The storm will return."

We hear steps behind us, and two more fishermen come out from the shadows, lifting a rope net between them. One mutters, "It's the Lost-and-Founder," and the other replies, "Aye, Herbert Lemon is here."

Yet more fishermen appear, some from the pub itself, others climbing the slimy green steps from the beach, blocking our way. In a moment, without any real warning or chance to prepare, we are surrounded.

WIDDERSHINS CAT

THE THING ABOUT THE FISHERMEN of Eerie-on-
Sea is that they all look the same to me. Think heavy-
knit pullovers, waterproof jackets and beards you could
hide hedgehogs in, and you'd be most of the way there.
The only one who really stands out is Boadicea Bates,
and that's mostly because she has a less impressive beard
than the rest, being a woman and all. But what she lacks
in chin whiskers she more than makes up for with a wiry
black mane that probably eats hairbrushes for breakfast.
As head of the Bates family – the biggest fishing clan for
miles around – she's also the nearest thing the fishermen
have to a leader. It's Boadicea Bates herself who steps out
of the pub last and fixes me with a sailor's salt-sore eye.

"So, Herbert Lemon, I hear you have been entrusted

with something that belongs to us."

"Er…" I begin.

"An ancient stoppered bottle," Boadicea continues, as if there might be some doubt over what we're talking about, "in the shape of a fish."

"Ah!" I reply, switching on my best grin. "Well, the thing is—"

"And you have come to do the right thing," Boadicea states, nodding to the others. "You have seen the danger to the town, and you are here to return to us what is ours according to our ancient rights."

"Um…"

"Except we don't see it about your person, Herbert Lemon." Boadicea Bates's brow lowers threateningly. "*Our* bottle. Though I expect you'll be home to fetch it presently, isn't that right?"

"…" is all I can say now. The grin is coming loose and wobbling badly.

"In fact," adds Boadicea, beckoning to the fishermen holding the old net, "I expect we could speed things up mightily by carrying you straight home to get it now."

The curved wall of fishermen closes around us, with a grumble of leathery scowls. The net is raised over our heads.

The grin, which was probably a bad idea from the start, finally falls off my face and curls up to die somewhere between my feet. I feel Violet press in beside me as we are backed against the wall.

I'm just about to try the "Look over there!" trick and make a run for it when Erwin does something strange. He jumps off the sea wall, walks into the space between us and the fishermen, and then slowly – but very definitely – turns a complete circle, anticlockwise. There's an intake of breath from the fishermen, and they shuffle back, lowering the net. Erwin doesn't even look up at them as he begins to turn a second leisurely circle, in the same direction. I glance at Violet. Her face lights up with understanding as she watches the cat.

"A second turn!" cries Boadicea Bates as Erwin does indeed come back around to face the sailors again. "Bad omen is upon us!"

For a moment it looks as though Erwin has had enough of circles and is going to sit. He lowers his fuzzy bottom slowly towards the cobbles, and we can almost hear the straining lungs of the fishermen as they prepare to breathe a sigh of relief. But then, just as the tension reaches its peak, Erwin raises his backside again and – very carefully and deliberately – begins to turn a third anti-clockwise circle.

The effect on the sailors is electric.

They begin smacking their lips and making "Here, kitty, here!" noises.

They begin winding their hands around *clockwise*, in a way that's clearly meant to coax Erwin to change direction.

Those who have pieces of rope in their hands begin twitching them on the ground, saying, "Ahoy, cat!" and, "Moggy want a mousie?"

Erwin pauses in his turning and flicks one ear at this extraordinary pantomime. At this the fishermen double their efforts, their lips smacking and ropes twitching, and I really wish I had a camera – I've never seen anything like it.

"Come *on*!" Violet hisses to me. With all the fuss around Erwin, the threatening circle of seafarers has broken up, and there's a gap for us. We dart away and out onto the harbour wall, and in a moment we have run down half its length.

Looking back, we see that Erwin has begun moving along the promenade, away from us. The knot of fishermen, still doing all they can to stop the cat from completing his third anti-clockwise circle, go after him.

"What was all that about?" I say. But Violet can't answer because she's laughing too hard.

"Clever old Erwin!" she manages to get out eventually, when she gets her breath back. Then she puts on an exaggerated old sailor voice: *"When Eerie cat turns widdershins thrice, 'tis dreary luck for men and mice."*

"What?"

"Or something like that, anyway." Violet grins. "It's another old Eerie saying. I know because with so many fishermen coming up to the book dispensary over the last few days, I've heard every old wives' tale going. That's why I started reading up about it. The fishermen are extremely superstitious."

"But what was Erwin doing? And what's a widdershin?"

"*Widdershins* is just an old word meaning anti-clockwise," Violet replies. "Erwin was about to bring bad luck crashing down on us all, and the fishermen will do anything to stop that. They've probably gone to get a bucket of sardines to bribe him. As I said, clever old puss."

"Couldn't they just pick him up or something?" I ask.

"No," says Vi, slipping back into her piratical voice, "because *he who touches Bad Luck Cat will nary catch a cod nor sprat!*"

"You're making these up now."

But Violet shakes her head as she dissolves into laughter again.

"Anyway," I say, as I'm clearly the only one fit to say it, "it's just as well Erwin was there. I should have known the pub would be a risky place to be near, with this whole fish-bottle business going on. The fishermen practically own the Whelk & Walrus. We'll have to be careful going back."

The harbour wall has always been a battered old thing, and the relentless storm hasn't done it any favours. The wind gets gustier as we head further out, and we have to be careful of the edge. On one side of the wall, the sea rolls dark and cold and stretches out as far as the eye can see into Eerie Bay. I feel a wobble come into my legs.

A couple of fishermen on the deck of a big, ugly iron boat moored to the harbour wall glare at us as we pass. They are fiddling with something hidden beneath a tarpaulin and clearly don't want an audience.

"Come on," I say, leading Violet on.

"That's a huge fishing boat," Violet whispers, glancing back.

"It's the *Bludgeon*," I explain. "Boadicea Bates's boat. The biggest for miles around."

"Are you sure this is where we'll find Blaze Westerley?" Violet asks. "On one of these boats?"

"Yes, but not just any boat," I reply. "The Westerleys' vessel stands out from the rest."

At the end of the harbour wall a grizzled old fisherman sits on a lobster pot, whittling a tiny stick with a knife the size of a cutlass. I do my best not to make eye contact, but I distinctly hear his whiskers bristling as we approach. Perhaps if I could take off my Lost-and-Founder's cap I wouldn't be so easy to recognize, but I can hardly do that now, not with the incredible thing I have hiding under there. I dread to think what the fishermen would do to me if they find out that I've opened their precious bottle and let the electrical fairy out. But maybe Blaze can help me get rid of it.

"Is it this one?" says Violet, snapping me out of my thoughts. "Blaze Westerley's boat?"

And it is.

Below us, tied to an iron ring, is the most extraordinary vessel you're ever likely to see.

JORNTY SPARK

OLD SQUINT WESTERLEY is famously eccentric, but even if you'd never heard the strange stories they tell about him, you'd know he was odd just by looking at his crazy boat.

The *Jornty Spark* must have started out as a normal fishing vessel. It's still got the short, deep hull – painted mid-morning blue – and proud little wheelhouse that most of the older Eerie boats possess. But there the normalness ends.

I'm not talking about the wires, dials and widgets that festoon the control panel. I'm not even talking about the immense curved tusk that is strapped to the prow and covered in scrimshaw carvings. No, I'm talking about the mast. Or, rather, the place where once a mast would have been. In this place, the *Jornty Spark* sports something else entirely.

"A windmill?" says Violet. "Is that really a windmill?"

I nod. "Well, more a wind turbine."

At the top of a tall wooden pylon, four blades spin with a furious whine in the wind. With the boat itself below us in the water, the wind turbine is at our level, and its spinning sails are an impressive sight.

"Old Squint," I say, "has built Eerie-on-Sea's first – and so far only – electrical fishing boat."

"Pah!" comes a grumble from the grizzled old fisherman behind us. "It ain't natural. Wrong sort of sails for a boat."

"Let's go down and see if Blaze is on board," says Violet, ignoring the man and turning to lower herself down rungs in the harbour wall. But I stop her.

"Er, no!" I declare. "I don't do boats, remember?"

"Even if they're tied up and not going anywhere?"

But I ignore the question. In any case, it's not polite to board someone's boat without permission.

"Ahoy!" I call down, feeling a bit silly, because it isn't every day I get to shout "Ahoy!" "Ahoy there, *Jornty Spark*!"

A head pops out of the wheelhouse – a head with a flop of red hair over a pair of welding goggles. The goggles are raised, and the wary face of Blaze Westerley looks up.

"You're the boy from the hotel," he calls over the wind and the whine of the turbine. "The Lost-and-Founder. The one who took the fish-shaped bottle. What do *you* want?"

It's not exactly the response I was expecting.

"Um," I call down. "I was just ..."

"... just making enquiries," Violet shouts down for me. "And I'm Violet Parma, from the Eerie Book Dispensary, who's helping him. Of all the people in Eerie-on-Sea, we think you might know the most about that old bottle. Can you come up, please, so we can talk about it?"

Blaze glares at me. Then he looks at Violet. In a moment he scampers up the rungs and stands awkwardly in front of us.

"What's to talk about?" he says. "Are you going to give me the bottle or not?"

"I really like your boat," says Vi, dodging right past the tricky question as only Violet can do. "Herbie was just telling me it's electric. Did your uncle really build it? He must be very clever."

Blaze's eyes flash, but not so much with anger as with pride.

"Aye, he did. Custom-built engine, deep-storage battery, eighty horsepower of pure electrical drive, when she's up to speed."

"That sounds … fast?"

"Fast?" cries Blaze. "You've never heard of the *Jornty Spark*? This is the ship that made the Kessel Island run in less than twelve minutes. I don't think there's a ship faster in Eerie Bay."

"Ship!" comes an incredulous cry, and we all turn to look at the grizzled old fisherman. His leathery face is creased up with amusement. "That old tiddler boat, a *ship*? I wouldn't give you twenty smackers for her, and even that be for the scrap. *Ship!*"

Blaze Westerley clenches his fists.

"She's fast enough for you, old man. Dare to race me?"

"A-ha-ha-harrrr!" The sailor throws his head back in laughter. "I'll race you any time you want, boy. I've seen you pootling around in the shallows. Your uncle's tub might have been fast enough when she still had canvas on her, but she's a dud'un now. Like Squint himself."

Then he picks up a piece of loose rope from the harbour wall and tosses it into the spinning sails of the wind turbine. The rope tangles around them immediately, and they grind to a halt.

"No!" cries Blaze.

"Oh, whoopsie," says the old sailor, picking his teeth with the little stick he's been whittling. "Like I said, wrong sort of sails for a boat." And with this he stands, slides the giant knife into his belt, and strolls away down the harbour wall, towards the town.

Blaze quivers all over with anger and frustration.

"But ... but she *is* fast," he cries, as if to the whole world. "She *is*. The *Spark*'s got what it takes where it matters. It's just... I don't..."

"It's OK," says Vi, touching the boy's arm. "Don't let him get to you."

"It's not just him," says Blaze. "It's all of them! The other fishermen have always laughed at us, ever since..."

"Since what?" asks Violet.

"But they'll be sorry –" Blaze shakes his skinny fist at the back of the fisherman – "when my uncle Squint gets back!"

"I thought Squint was lost," I say. "At sea?"

"Aye, he is." Blaze looks at his feet. "But he's been lost before and managed to find his way home. If he can do it again, I want to be out there, ready to pick him up."

"I didn't think anyone was going out to sea at the moment," Violet says. "I thought the storm was keeping all you fishermen grounded."

"It may keep *them* grounded," says Blaze, nodding back along the wall towards the Whelk & Walrus, "with their diesel engines and mouldy sails. But the *Spark's* different."

"Look, Blaze –" Violet rummages in her pocket – "that fish-shaped bottle has some strange symbols on it. What can you tell us about them?"

And she pulls out the piece of paper with the crayon rubbing on. She unfolds the paper and holds it up, flapping in the wind.

"Is it really some sort of secret writing?"

"Aye, it's the Eerie Script," Blaze replies. "It's a secret lost to time."

At least, this is what his mouth says. But the way he glances away and looks shifty says something else.

"Blaze?" says Vi, refolding the paper. "What happened to your uncle exactly? How did he get lost at sea?"

The teenager still seems torn between saying one thing and doing something else. In the end, he just mumbles, "You aren't fisherfolk. Neither of you. You wouldn't understand."

"I would love to understand," I tell him. "I really would. But in the meantime, what are we going to do about them?"

"Them?" say Blaze and Vi together.

"Yes," I squeak. *"Them!"*

And I point back along the harbour wall, to where a large group of men have gathered. A large group of fishermen, to be precise, with Boadicea Bates at the head. Beside her, the whittling sailor is pointing back our way. As we watch, the whole bunch of them begin a steady, menacing walk towards us, filling the entire width of the wall. With nothing but heaving sea in all other directions, they are completely blocking any escape. And behind them, watching from the doorway of the Whelk & Walrus, is the unmistakable figure of Deep Hood.

"Oh, bladderwracks!"

I feel a stirring under my cap as the little electrical creature gives a start.

"We're trapped!" says Violet.

I see her look at the waves, and I know her well enough to guess she's wondering what our chances would be if we made a swim for it. But for once even Violet judges something to be too dangerous.

"Trapped?" says Blaze. "You make it sound as if they're after you."

"They are!" I blurt out. "They think I should give

them the fish bottle. And they're not being very subtle about it."

"You mean you haven't?" says Blaze. "I thought that was why you'd come to the harbour. To hand it over to Boadicea and her cronies."

"No!" I say. "I haven't decided what to do with the stupid thing. But if you thought that, then maybe *they* think …"

"… maybe they think you're here to give it to *me*," Blaze completes the sentence. "Come on!"

"Come on, *what*?"

"They think they have you cornered," says the boy. "Only, they haven't reckoned on Uncle Squint's engine. I can't wait to see their faces when we're powering away from the harbour at maximum thrust."

"You mean…?" I start to say, not wanting to say any of it all.

"Aye!" cries Blaze Westerley. "All aboard! All aboard the *Jornty Spark*!"

OLD SQUINT'S ENGINE

BLAZE IS THE FIRST TO REACH the deck of his boat, and he immediately sets about untying it from the harbour wall. Violet stops halfway down the ladder and looks up at me.

"Herbie, come on!"

But I don't "come on!" How can I, when "coming on" means doing a thing I said I'd never do again?

I think back to when I first told Violet the story of how I washed up in Eerie-on-Sea in a crate of lemons. I remember how impressed I was that she didn't laugh at the lemons part. In fact, she didn't laugh at any of it – not the bit where Mrs Fossil (who else?) found me half drowned on the beach, or where Dr Thalassi got the seawater out of my lungs (yikes, I'll never forget that!). She didn't even smirk at the part where Lady Kraken took me in, and gave me a job and a uniform and my unlikely name. Which is why it's so annoying when I look down at Violet now, beckoning me onto the boat, and see the glint of amusement in her eyes. She's probably one of those people who believes in facing up to your fears, isn't she? Yes, of course she is.

"Herbert Lemon!"

That's Boadicea Bates calling that, roaring into the wind from the head of the gang of approaching fishermen.

"We have things to say to you, boy."

And so I'm faced with a choice: get on the boat – despite the mermonkey's warning – and run the risk of a watery end on the cold, dark bottom of the sea, or *don't* get on the boat, and face the certainty of being nabbed by a bunch of angry fishermen with ropes and knives.

I hurry down the ladder.

Well, at least this should only be a short trip.

The *Jornty Spark* is already moving away from the quayside as Blaze shoves an urgent oar against the wall, so I'm forced to jump.

"Argh!" I cry, hitting the rolling deck and waving my arms to keep balance. "Wait for me!"

"Stop complaining and get that rope off the turbine,"

Blaze barks in return, his shy awkwardness gone as he gives the order. He grabs a tatty skipper's cap from the top handgrip of the wheel and jams it onto his head. "We can't engage the engine while the pylon's up, and I can't lower it while the turbine's tangled."

I look up at the wind turbine above us. Viewed from the deck, it suddenly seems ridiculously high. I step towards it, but the boat chooses that moment to lean sharply. I let out a groan and clutch a brass handgrip on the wheelhouse. There's a sudden twinge in my scalp, as I feel the strange little creature under my cap respond to my alarm. The deck tips even further, and everything loose slides across it.

"We need to get that pylon down!" cries Blaze, leaning out over the water, using his weight to correct the boat's balance. We're away from the harbour wall now and turning out of control. "The turbine makes us top-heavy."

"Herbie!" Violet cries, leaning out beside Blaze to help him, but there's nothing I can do – my legs are rooted to the spot with fear.

The wind shifts, and suddenly the boat is swinging back the other way.

Violet wastes no time. She jumps forward and

shimmies up the pylon like a cat, reaching the top just as it teeters momentarily upright. She scrabbles at the rope, pulling it away in frantic loops. The coils fall to the deck, as the deck starts to tip the other way.

Blaze darts over to my side of the boat and swings out over the water again, holding on by just his finger and boot tips in a desperate attempt to counter the weight of the turbine now that a girl is on top of it.

Violet slides down the pylon – her boots hitting the deck with a bang.

Blaze immediately jumps into the wheelhouse and starts jabbing at switches. With a *clack!* the wooden blades of the turbine fold down, no longer presenting a windmill to the wind. Then, with a steady clanking sound, the pylon begins to lower towards the deck of the boat.

On the harbour wall above, beyond the cry of the seagulls and the harsh gusting of the wind, comes a roar of fury from Boadicea.

"Blaze Westerley! Bring that Lost-and-Founder back here. He has something that belongs to us."

This prompts a grumble of angry agreement from the fishermen gathered on the harbour wall.

"He's aboard the *Spark* now," Blaze calls back, the

skipper's cap firmly on his head, "and has the protection of the Westerleys."

With the pylon lowered there is less seesaw pressure on the boat. But I'm still clutching the handgrip.

"Herbie, it's OK," says Violet.

Is it? I want to shout. But I can't do anything right now but cling on.

"Think of the town!" comes the voice of Boadicea Bates again, carrying across the growing distance between us and dry land. "Eerie is in danger. No matter how crazy your uncle was, you Westerleys are an old fishing family. You know the lore and our ancient rights. That fish-shaped bottle is a Dismal business, and the property of *all* us fisherfolk. You must bring it to us."

"It's my uncle's business!" Blaze calls back. "And I will not let you have it." And then, turning to us, he adds, "Brace yourselves. I'm going to engage the engine."

"Do you think they'll try to follow?" asks Vi, planting her feet firmly on the deck and grabbing the rail.

"They think they won't need to," I cry. "Look!"

Back on the harbour wall, one fisherman has stepped apart from the others. He starts to twirl a rope, tied into a lasso. There are dozens of things on Blaze's modified boat that it could catch on, not least of which the great curving tusk on the prow, and we're still drifting without any power.

Blaze grabs a key on the control panel.

He turns it.

There's a wheezing, whining sound, and several dials on the control panel light up. A large dial in the centre, with the word CHARGE on it, flickers with a quivering blue light, its needle trembling at the zero mark.

The fisherman throws his lasso with the precision of a man who has done such things all his life. The loop sails through the air towards us, as the dial finally lights up a solid blue. The needle slams over from zero to max, and the *Jornty Spark*'s engine roars into life.

Blaze pushes, hard, on the drive lever.

We are flung back with sudden acceleration. Violet and I cling to the rail, and Blaze to his wheel, as the motor thrusts us forward at incredible speed, showering us with spray. The rope lasso misses the back of the boat by a finger's width and falls behind us into the churning water.

Violet gives a whoop of triumph as we race away.

"Yes!" cries Blaze, his skipper's cap blowing off his head. "I got her working again! Oh, see, Uncle, see! I told you I was ready. I fixed the engine!"

But then, just as quickly as it started, the tremendous acceleration stops, and the roar of the motor dies away. The blue lights on the control panel flicker out as the needle of the dial drops back to near zero. The water that was spraying up behind the *Jornty Spark* as she sliced through the sea is soon replaced by some very modest ripples.

"No!" cries Blaze, pulling back the drive lever and thrusting it forward again, repeatedly but uselessly. "No, not again!"

"What happened?" says Vi.

"Here, take the wheel!"

It's me he's talking to. My hands fly out automatically. And now I'm holding the wheel of an actual real-life boat, exactly as if a mechanical monkey with a mermaid's tail has never dispensed me a copy of *The Cold, Dark Bottom of the Sea* by Sebastian Eels.

Blaze slams up a hatch in the wheelhouse floor and jumps down into the dark beyond. An oily and electrical tang wafts out from the hatchway.

"We're still moving, aren't we?" says Vi, joining me at the wheel.

Somehow I manage to nod. We are moving, just very, *very* slowly. The boat bobs in the rolling sea, seeming smaller and more fragile the further we get from shore.

"So much for the fastest boat in Eerie Bay," Violet says, and sighs. "But at least we've put some distance between us and them."

I look back at the quayside.

The fishermen are still there, watching in silent menace as we make our low-speed escape to nowhere. In the other direction, across a horizon black with storm, a bolt of lightning tears across the sky.

We're on the rolling sea, in a boat with almost no power, heading towards the greatest storm anyone in Eerie has ever known. And I suddenly realize that the nearest land is straight down – down on the cold, dark seabed below.

THE SEAFARER'S
APPRENTICE

THERE'S A GREAT DEAL of banging and clanging coming from down below the hatchway, and a lot of very colourful seafarer language.

"Blaze?" Violet calls through the hatch in alarm. "What's happening?"

A head appears, blackened with engine grease and topped with waving red hair raised by static. Blaze Westerley pulls himself up onto the deck, slumps beside the wheel and flings down a spanner.

"It's no good," he declares. "I can't fix it. Uncle Squint was right. I'm just not ready."

Violet and I exchange a look.

"If the battery only charges from the windmill," I say, trying out my helpful voice, even though I'm not really in the mood, "maybe it just needs more time. The turbine isn't *that* big."

"It's been charging for days!" Blaze throws up his hands. "With all the wind from the storm, the battery should be bursting with power. *I'm* the problem, not the engine."

"Herbie's good at fixing things," says Violet brightly. "Maybe he could take a look."

"Him!" Blaze glares at me. "It would take a nautical genius to understand Uncle Squint's engine. All *he's* done since he's come aboard is make squeaking noises and turn green."

I'm annoyed by this. I feel my face go red (not green), and underneath my cap the hidden light crackles with stinging sparks. I should just take my cap off. That'll give Blaze something to talk about!

"Herbie hasn't been on a boat for a while, that's all," Violet says, avoiding my eyes. "Besides, he's doing his best. And Herbie's best is better than a lot of people's."

Blaze stares at his boots. Then he lets out a sigh.

"Must be nice," he mumbles to me, "to hear something like that."

I'm not sure if this is supposed to be an apology, but it seems as though pretending that it is will help the situation. I pick up the fallen skipper's cap and give it to

Blaze. He takes it, but he doesn't put it on.

"I can't promise anything," I say, curiosity getting the better of me, "but I'd love to see Squint Westerley's engine anyway."

Blaze gets to his feet and presses a switch to lock the wheel.

"We'll be safe out at sea for a while yet," he says.

Then he indicates the hatchway with a bob of his head.

I straighten my Lost-and-Founder's cap, pull the front of my uniform flat and lower myself down into the hull of the *Jornty Spark*.

It's dark down here. The air is heavy and close and smells like spent fireworks. There's a small galley kitchen, crazily cluttered with kettles and plates and signs of an unfinished breakfast of toast and eggs. Two hammocks swing with the motion of the sea, and in the light of four portholes, I spot a shelf of well-thumbed books and lots of charts and papers pinned to the wall. Above all these, like a totem, is a dog-eared postcard of Saint Dismal. The old saint scowls at us with a stormy expression, the star bright over his head.

"You live down here?" says Violet to Blaze as they

both join me. "You and your uncle?"

"Aye," says Blaze, ducking to avoid clonking his head on the low ceiling. "There's bags of room really."

But I'm not paying attention. Even my discomfort at being at sea is forgotten as I stare at the object that fills the back half of the area below deck.

Hulking in the gloom is a mass of gleaming green ceramic, braced against the hull by girders wrapped in rubber. Along the back of this extraordinary object are two rows of glass domes, each filled with copper coils in a faintly glowing liquid. The whole thing is festooned with bunches of wire that emerge from one place, only to loop around and re-enter somewhere else. It's a battery, it has to be, though it's like no battery I've ever seen. The air around it feels stiff with electrical charge, and beyond it lies the aluminium casing of the powerful electric motor that drives the boat.

"I can't fix this," I say eventually. "This is bonkers. Your *uncle* built this?"

"Took him years."

"I'm starting to think," I reply, "that he really was a genius."

"Yup." Blaze rubs a smudge of oil from his nose and looks proud.

"But … why?" Violet says.

"Why what?"

"Why did he build an electric engine?"

Blaze stares at us both a moment, before throwing a quick glance at the papers and sketches on the wall.

"He had his reasons."

Violet walks over to a big chart pinned up in the galley. It shows Eerie Bay in its entirety, with the town just a detail on the coast. The chart is very old and has handwritten notes all over it. As Violet peers at these closely, she gasps.

"Eerie Script!" she declares, jabbing at the paper. "Some of this is written in Eerie Script. Like on the side of the bottle. Look, Herbie!"

"What's that?" I say, spotting a peculiar swirl drawn on the map. There are several messages near by in Eerie Script.

"That," says Blaze, "is the Vortiss."

"The *What*-iss?"

"The Vortiss. Haven't you heard of it?" The teenager looks surprised. "No, I suppose you wouldn't have, not being fisherfolk."

Then his voice suddenly sounds much older, as if he's repeating something told to him many times.

"Deep in the furthest reaches of Maw Rocks, where no chart can be trusted, there's a place where we fishermen must never go. The currents are terrible and combine to a neverending and inescapable whirlpool known as the Vortiss."

Blaze spirals his fingertip around and around the drawing on the chart as he speaks.

"They say there are strange lights and treacherous winds there. They say it's the place where storms are born. Lightning will explode a diesel engine, and the wind will shred your sails. Either way, it's a quick drowning for any who approach it, so none ever do, by order of Saint Dismal himself. I doubt there's a fisherman alive who's even clapped eyes on the Vortiss and lived to tell it. Except…"

"Old Squint Westerley." Violet's voice is a near-whisper. "Your uncle."

Blaze nods.

"And you?"

The shyness comes back over the boy, and he says nothing.

"Blaze, please tell us what happened," says Violet. "What's Squint's story? Why did he sail to the Vortiss? And what's the connection with Gargantis?"

Blaze's head snaps up.

"Who said there's a connection with *that*?"

"You did," says Vi. "By the way you just reacted."

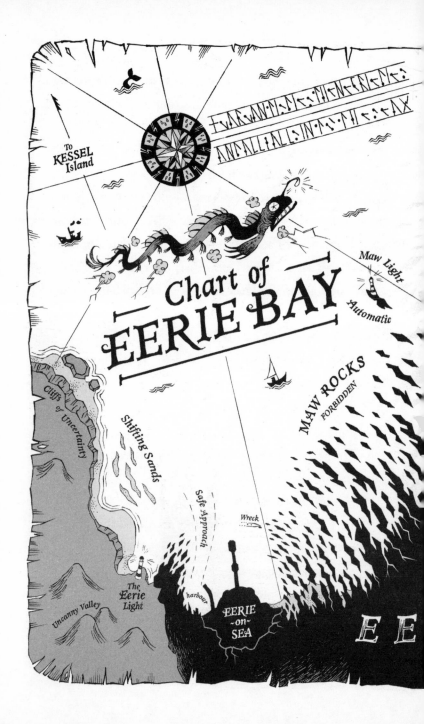

"It started years ago." Blaze leans back into a hammock. "Long before I became his apprentice. My uncle was just one of the regular fisherfolk then, like generations before him, trawling the bay for a net of mackerel, and bringing in a garshark or a gazbaleen when his luck was in. Out in all weathers by day, and then down the Whelk & Walrus by night, telling tall tales of the one that got away over pints of Clammy Dodger. It would have been a good life for a fisherman, if it hadn't been for one thing."

"What thing?"

"Curiosity."

"Curiosity?" Violet and I say together.

"Aye," says Blaze. "Uncle Squint was riddled with it. It wasn't enough to make a good catch, he had to know the *how* and the *why* of it. He wanted to *understand*. But we fisherfolk don't need to understand, that's what Boadicea Bates said. We just need to follow the laws of Saint Dismal, as we've always done. And no law is more strict than the one forbidding us to approach the Vortiss."

"But why did your uncle want to do that?" Vi asks.

"Fish have always been more plentiful around Maw Rocks," says Blaze. "Uncle just wanted to know why, and to see the Vortiss for himself. So he began exploring. Just a little at first, but soon he was sailing deeper and deeper into the maze of rocks, battling the currents. Then one day, he went too deep. Terrible winds engulfed him, and strange lightning, and the *Jornty* – she was just the *Jornty* back then, with canvas sails – lost her mast. Uncle was swept overboard and swallowed into the swirling mouth of the Vortiss.

"They found the *Jornty* the next day, drifting far out in the open sea, battered and barely afloat. But of Squint Westerley there was no sign – he was lost for good. Or so everyone thought."

"He came back?"

Blaze nods.

"A few days later, he crawled up onto the beach. He was in a terrible state. They carried him to the pub and brought him back to life with brandy and a slap. They were agog to hear his story, so he told them there and then a strange tale of an underwater world beneath Eerie Rock, where lie the wrecks of all the ships the Vortiss has gobbled up over hundreds of years. And the skeletons of all the men who were gobbled with them, too. And there was something else. Something huge. Something coiled in the deepest part of the cavern."

"Something?" I manage to say, my throat suddenly dry.

"Yes," says Blaze. "Something monstrous."

SOMETHING MONSTROUS

"IT WAS THAT PART OF HIS STORY that made the others laugh at him." Blaze thrusts his hands into his pockets and looks angry. "They said Uncle had gone too far with his tall tales this time, that the only person who ever survived the Vortiss was Saint Dismal himself, and then only by a miracle. No one in Eerie-on-Sea has taken Uncle Squint seriously since."

"But when you say 'monstrous'," asks Vi, "what do you mean, exactly?"

Blaze shrugs.

"The more people laughed, the less Squint talked about it. Even to me." Then he points at the little shelf of books, piled higgledy-piggledy above the stove. "But the less he talked, the more he read. He'd go up to the book dispensary in the town, to get more books."

"Wait!" Vi's eyes flash. "These books were chosen for your uncle by the mermonkey?"

Blaze nods.

"The more he read, the less time he spent fishing. It didn't stop him exploring Maw Rocks, though. He began mapping them, updating the old charts, understanding the currents. And then he had the idea to build this electrical engine. He became obsessed with reaching the Vortiss again."

"There are books here about weather –" Violet pokes around the bookshelf – "about local legends, and electrical engineering, and—"

"Do *you* believe him?" I blurt out over Violet. "About the monstrous something at the bottom of the sea, and the *skeletons*?"

Blaze glares at me from under his flop of hair.

"If my uncle said there were skeletons, there were skeletons."

I close my eyes and try not to think of the white figures falling into the abyss on the cover of *The Cold, Dark Bottom of the Sea* by Sebastian Eels. But the boat rolls sharply, and I can't help thinking about them anyway.

"Besides," Blaze adds, "Uncle didn't come back empty-handed. He came back with proof of what he'd seen."

"What proof?" says Vi.

"Surely you've seen it," Blaze says. "On the prow of the *Jornty Spark*? The tusk? It's massive! It's not the tusk of any known animal. At least, so people say."

"Do you think I could copy these?" Violet asks Blaze then, pointing at the inscriptions in Eerie Script on the chart. She gets her big piece of paper out of her pocket.

"Aye, go ahead." He shrugs. "I'm more interested in getting this blasted engine fixed."

And he gives the great ceramic battery a kick. There's a flicker, and electrical light shimmers through the glass domes, but the engine remains sluggish.

"You haven't told us what happened to Squint in the end," Violet says as she draws. "How did he drown?"

Blaze blows the hair out of his eyes.

"The truth is, Uncle was struggling to finish the engine. We aren't rich, and he kept running out of money and parts. But then, a few weeks ago, a stranger came to the harbour wall and offered to help."

"A stranger?" I say. "What sort of stranger?"

Blaze shrugs again.

"The strangest kind. I never saw his face clearly. He always kept it hidden in the shadows of a deep hood."

Violet and I exchange looks.

"But Uncle agreed. Suddenly there was gold to spend, and the work got finished. After years of tinkering and test runs, the new electrical *Jornty Spark* was complete, and it ran like a dream. We were finally ready for our trip to the Vortiss. The stranger wanted just one thing in return."

"Yes?"

"He wanted to go with us."

"To the Vortiss?" Violet says. "And Squint accepted this?"

"Why shouldn't he?" says Blaze. "My uncle was the only person who knew how to get there, and thanks to this stranger's money, he finally had a boat that could make the voyage too. It seemed a fair exchange. They made the deal and the stranger came aboard. After a few preparations, we set out."

"So what happened?"

"We entered Maw Rocks from the north. The channels are wider there, and the currents are easier to navigate, at least at first. The *Spark* was battered by ferocious winds, but we had no sails to rip. Strange sparks of lightning circled us and danced along the hull, but we had no diesel engines to explode. And so, we came to the Vortiss. Then, with the engines roaring and the wheel locked to keep position, I lowered my uncle, and our passenger, into the sea in a barrel."

"What?" we both cry.

"That was the plan!" Blaze shouts back defensively. "The deal we made. Only…"

"Only something went wrong?" says Vi.

Blaze gives a desperate nod.

"The barrel was halfway to the whirlpool when the two men started fighting. Uncle had his axe out, and I didn't know what to do. I was just about to winch them in again when the man in the hood got an arm free and threw something at the *Spark*. You're going to find this hard to believe, but I think it was a bomb."

"A *bomb*?"

"It landed in the water close by and went off with an almighty bang. I was thrown to the deck. By the time I got up again, the barrel, Uncle Squint and the man in the hood were all gone, the rope cut clean through. They were swallowed by the Vortiss!"

"Down to the cold, dark—" I start to say, but Violet nudges me in the ribs.

"Bits of the explosion got into the *Spark*'s engine," Blaze continues, his eyes wet and wide as he stares into the memory. "Everything went haywire! I managed to go full reverse, and get out of the currents, but the battery began to lose power. It took me hours to get home. Hours to think about Uncle Squint …"

Blaze clenches his fists.

"… and how I lost him!"

Just then there's a jolt. The boat shudders and tips alarmingly.

"What's that?" Violet says, clutching the bookshelf as the boat continues to tip. "It almost feels like … like something heavy is…"

There's another jolt, and the boat creaks as the back end of it is pulled down even further.

Blaze snaps out of his despair.

"Someone's climbing aboard!" he exclaims. "Pulling themselves out of the sea!"

Then he runs for the ladder and scurries up it.

"I'm coming, Uncle! I'm coming! I knew you'd find your way back!"

We rush after him, as the boat continues to tip. But when we get out on deck and see what is heaving itself onto the *Jornty Spark*, we know immediately that it isn't Squint Westerley.

THE LAST OF
THE WESTERLEYS

THE FIRST THING WE SEE is a tentacle.

A glistening pink tentacle that is wrapped around
the brass railing at the back of the boat, suckering onto it
and heaving up some great weight.

"An octopus!" cries Violet, clutching my arm.

I rub my eyes in terrified disbelief.

How can there be an octopus?

But when I look again, there is no tentacle, no octopus
at all, just a powerful human arm. And then another,
followed by a leg.

The owner of these limbs drags himself aboard, and
a tall, ghastly figure stands erect on the deck of the *Jornty
Spark*, streaming with seawater. One hand is clutching
the handle of a metal-bound box that I've seen before,

while the other hand is rising towards us. Where his face should be is nothing but the shadow of a hood.

"Herbert Lemon," Deep Hood drawls in his disgusting voice. "I know what you took from the bottle."

I clutch my cap and stagger back into the wheelhouse, Violet at my side.

"Herbert Lemon," Deep Hood burbles on, "give it to me!"

"You!" cries Blaze, suddenly finding his voice. "You're the stranger, the one we took to the Vortiss. The one who fought my uncle. You survived!"

Deep Hood hisses at the boy, and then steps towards him. Blaze snatches up the spanner he dropped earlier.

"It's all your fault Uncle's gone!" Blaze cries, and he leaps forward, the spanner raised like a club.

There's a flash of pink, and something whips out from Deep Hood, smashing Blaze in the face. In a moment, Blaze is lying on his back, groaning, the spanner clattering across the deck and falling into the sea.

And now Deep Hood is advancing again, one arm raised, pointing directly at me.

"Give it to me, Herbert Lemon!"

Under my cap, the hair on my head starts to rise as a massive electrical charge builds, as if the little fairy thing I have hidden there is feeding on my terror.

"Give it to me," gurgles Deep Hood, "or I will drag you to your doom on the cold, dark bottom of the sea."

And he makes a noise that sounds like laughing.

My cap explodes.

Literally, it blows off with a *twang!* of slipped elastic and a *KA-CHA-BOOM!* of localized thunder. A bright bolt of lightning leaps from my head and connects with Deep Hood's outstretched hand. The man is engulfed in brilliant light and hurled backwards, his coat flying. Myriad arcs of power crackle along the railing of the *Jornty Spark*, as Deep Hood topples over it and hits the sea with an almighty splash.

There's a moment of astonished silence in the wheelhouse.

My cap lands back on the deck with a soft thud.

Then, above us, the dials of the control deck light up a steady blue.

"There's charge in the battery!" Violet shouts, jumping to her feet.

She slams the drive lever forward.

With a powerful roar and a plume of water, we leap ahead and surge away from the terrible figure who just boarded us, and out into the open sea.

"Is he following?" I shout over the engine's whine.

It's a few minutes later, and Violet and I are looking fearfully over our shoulders. The empty sea churns behind us as we power through the water.

"I don't know," Violet replies. "I … I don't think so."

"There was a moment," I gasp, "when we first saw him, when he seemed to have … to have…"

"A tentacle?" Violet says in a whisper.

"He *can't* have," I say. "And yet, you saw it too?"

The sound of the engine drops as Violet pulls the throttle back. She runs to the back of the boat and starts scanning the rolling sea.

There's a groan, and I help Blaze to his feet.

"What … what hit me?" he says groggily.

"It was some kind of whip," Violet says. "Yes, it must have been. Some kind of whip that Deep Hood keeps under his coat. And he must have used it to board us, after swimming out here."

But Blaze doesn't reply. He's staring at me open-mouthed, a look of amazement on his face.

It's then I remember that I'm no longer wearing my Lost-and-Founder's cap.

"A sprightning!" Blaze gasps, pointing over my head. "You have … a sprightning!"

"I do?"

Over me, the little electrical fairy is flitting around in a sparkling glow, just above my head. Then it settles down into my hair, and I feel it curling around and around, like Erwin does when he's trying to get comfortable.

Violet passes me my cap.

"It was in the fish-shaped bottle," she explains. "And we, um, we sort of let it out."

"But it's a *sprightning*!" Blaze cries.

"Whatever it is," I say, taking the cap, "it seems to have latched on to me, sparks and all. I can't make it go away."

"What is a sprightning anyway?" asks Violet.

"I don't really know," Blaze confesses, "but my uncle does. We saw some near the Vortiss, though none as big as yours. He said they can be extremely dangerous."

"Good for us that they are," Violet replies, with a grin of relief. "Not so good for Deep Hood!"

"Don't be so sure," says Blaze. "If that sprightning was in the bottle, and the fishermen find out you've taken it, it won't be good for any of us. Uncle always said…"

Then he stops and blinks, and I wonder if his brains are still rattled from the bash in the face. Mine would be.

But it can't be that, because he cries again, "My uncle!"

"What about him?"

"If the stranger in the hood survived, then my uncle might have too!" Blaze grabs Violet's shoulders and starts dancing her around. "He's really out there. He's alive!"

"OK, OK…" Violet dances around with Blaze once, then calms him down. "I'm sure he is. But you'll need to get the engine running again, won't you? To go and look for him?"

Blaze nods and jams the skipper's cap onto his head. He runs to the wheelhouse and starts flipping switches.

"How's the battery doing?" I ask, eager to change the subject. Eerie-on-Sea is large on the horizon, but not large enough for my liking. I'd give a month's worth of stale croissants to get back on dry land right now.

"Something's still not right," Blaze says, taking the wheel again and adjusting a dial. "Despite that boost, we're already losing power."

Sure enough, the needle on the dial is steadily dropping back towards zero.

"Do you think…?" He turns to look at me, or rather

at the glowing thing that has nestled into my hair. "Do you think you could do that again? Another zap would be useful."

Very carefully, I reach up and scoop the little sprightning into my hands. It's sleeping now, curled up in a warm glow in my palms.

"It's not me who does the zaps," I say, gently putting the dozing sprite back into my hair and carefully replacing my cap. "I think you'll have to fix the engine the old-fashioned way."

Blaze sighs. His hands dart expertly across the control panel, flipping switches and tweaking knobs, but the needle keeps falling.

"If only I could," he says. "I just don't get what's wrong with it."

"Really?" asks Violet. "Are you so sure? You look like you know what you're doing to me."

Blaze says nothing for a moment. Then:

"Well, I … I did wonder if it might be the flow capacitor. Back when the explosion happened – at the Vortiss, I mean – bits of metal pierced the hull and hit the battery. It's possible that the polarity of the flow capacitor got flipped."

"I don't know what any of that means," Violet replies.

"But it sounds like you do. Have you checked?"

Blaze stares at her.

"I can't reverse the polarity of a flow capacitor! I'm only an apprentice."

"When I first became Lost-and-Founder at the Grand Nautilus Hotel," I say into the silence that follows this, "I didn't have a clue what I was doing. Mr Mollusc said I was the worst Lost-and-Founder there had ever been, and I believed him. But after a bit, in my own way, it turned out…"

"What?"

"It turned out," Violet replies for me, "that Herbie knows more about lost-and-foundering than anyone. He can certainly run rings around that stuffy old Mollusc. So maybe, Blaze, you can do more than you know. Maybe your apprenticeship is already over, and you haven't realized it yet."

Blaze doesn't reply. But we can both tell he's thinking about it. And I wonder suddenly what more there is to know about Blaze Westerley. What's his own story? Why is he all alone on this boat, fending for himself?

Where are *his* parents?

I look out at the empty sea and think that perhaps we have more in common, this teenage fisherman and

I, than just learning on the job. I wonder what book the mermonkey would dispense for him.

"Maybe..." Blaze says eventually. "Maybe I'll take a look at that capacitor after all. Just in case."

And with another glance at my cap, he flips a switch, grips the wheel, and expertly guides the *Jornty Spark* towards home.

FRAZZLED

"WHERE WILL WE GO ASHORE?" Violet asks Blaze. "We'd like to avoid meeting any more fishermen, if possible."

"And Deep Hood!" I add.

"You do think he survived that blast of lightning, then?" Vi says.

I look out over the rolling, choppy sea.

"I think I don't want to count on anything except getting back to my Lost-and-Foundery and stoking up the wood burner," I reply.

"There's a place I know, near the cliffs," Blaze says. "I can get in close to the beach there, but you'll have to jump. Is that OK?"

"It's fine," Violet calls back. "Isn't it, Herbie?"

It's not, actually. But I'm so desperate to get off this boat that I nod anyway.

The *Spark* approaches the edge of Maw Rocks, where the sea stacks reach the shore. A slab of gleaming stone, studded with barnacles, breaks into view between waves. The beach is beyond it, strewn with chunks of driftwood, clumps of seaweed and storm-tossed detritus.

Blaze expertly eases us alongside the slab.

"This is as close as I can get," he says.

"What will you do now?" Vi asks, getting ready to jump.

"Go back to the harbour wall," Blaze replies. "Then..." He glances at each of us, as if for reassurance. "Then I guess I'll get back to work on the engine."

I do a nod. I hope it's an encouraging one.

"What will you do?" he asks in return. Then he nods at my cap. "What will you do with *that*?"

But I don't have an answer to this, not yet, so I say nothing.

Balancing as carefully as we can, Violet and I clamber over to the prow of the *Jornty Spark*, which is bobbing dangerously close to the rock. Violet pauses to look at the tusk that is strapped there so proudly, the tusk Squint Westerley claimed to have brought back from the Vortiss.

Then we jump ashore.

The *Jornty Spark* peels away from the rock, pushing back out into the rolling sea. Blaze raises his skipper's cap in farewell.

"So, what *do* we do next?"

It's Violet asking this, after we've climbed the shingle bank. She sits down on a rock, beside the sea-worn steps that lead up to the promenade. Above us looms the mighty ramparts of Eerie-on-Sea's castle.

"We're no closer to understanding the secret writing," I say, sitting beside her and enjoying the reassuring feel of solid stone beneath my bum. "And I've never heard of this Vortiss before. I don't know how anything Blaze told us helps me figure out what to do with that blasted fish-shaped bottle."

"But it's not the bottle that's important, is it, Herbie?" says Vi. "It's what was inside. Talking of which, how are things up there?" And she points at my cap.

I tip my head from side to side.

"All quiet," I reply. "For now. But I can't carry on like this, Vi. Someone's going to get hurt. Probably me!"

"Well, at least we've learned something useful,"

Violet says then, with a mischievous grin. "Something useful to *you*, anyway."

"Really?"

"You just went on a boat trip, Herbert Lemon, and we didn't sink. Do you still think that *The Cold, Dark Bottom of the Sea* by Sebastian Eels is a warning from the mermonkey?"

I look out across the rolling waves to the distant storm. We've just been chased by fishermen, attacked by a stranger armed with some kind of whip and nearly swept out into the open ocean in a boat with a broken engine. Frankly, I think we're lucky to be alive. Trust Violet to find something positive to say about it all.

"Maybe the best thing you could do right now, Herbie, is come to the book dispensary with me and consult the mermonkey again. A new book might just make everything clearer."

But I'm not ready to do that. I'm just about to say so, with knobs on, when a particularly loud crash of surf draws our attention back to the sea. Something has broken the surface of the water, near the shore.

"What's that?" says Violet.

It rises from the surf, the thing, seawater streaming off it.

Then it stands erect.

Deep Hood walks out of the sea, striding powerfully up the beach, his metal-bound box hanging at his side. We drop behind the rock we were sitting on.

The stranger crunches past us on the beach, making for the steps. Then he stops and turns. He swings his drooping hood from side to side with a horrible snorting breath, as if he's sniffing – sniffing for something.

Or someone.

Violet and I go completely still as seagulls cry overhead, and the surf crashes on the shore below.

Deep Hood sniffs a final time and then turns away, continuing his climb to the sea wall. We shrink closer to our rock, our faces pressed into the seaweed, as the awful man climbs the slippery steps above us, three at a time, up to Eerie-on-Sea.

It's a few minutes before we dare to move.

A seagull lands on the rock and peers at us hungrily.

"Hey!" says Violet, shooing the bird away. "We're not dead!"

Yet! I add, but only in my head.

Then we jump up and run to the steps. It feels risky to be stepping in the watery footsteps of Deep Hood so soon, but this is the quickest way to get off the beach.

And being on the beach is the surest way to get ourselves seen from above.

When we reach the top, we slip across the cobbles of the promenade and dart into the familiar, twisty old streets of Eerie-on-Sea.

It's then that a large hand clamps down on my shoulder.

MERMONKEY

I SPIN AROUND and see a familiar face looking down at me – an olive-coloured face with a pair of caterpillar eyebrows and an impressive Julius Caesar nose.

"Dr Thalassi!" I cry, relieved.

"Good morning, Herbie. Good morning, Violet," says the doc, raising his hat and surveying our crumpled and sea-spattered appearance. The doctor is wearing a waterproof coat and has several tools poking out of his pockets. "I was just out fixing storm damage on the castle roof when I saw you come ashore. So, you've been out on the *Jornty Spark*. And, er, spoken to Blaze Westerley?"

"I was on important Lost-and-Founder business," I say. "We thought he could tell us more about the fish-shaped bottle, and..."

"Ah!" says the doc, with an anxious waggle of his eyebrows. "And are you any closer to deciding who should get it? I hope you aren't tempted to give such a historically important relic to the Westerleys. I don't see how Blaze can have a good claim, despite what he says about his uncle."

"Herbie hasn't decided anything," Violet says firmly. "We just wanted to find out if Blaze knew anything about the secret writing. That's all."

"But if you wanted to know more about *that*, you should have come to me," replies the doc. "What are you doing now? Perhaps you'd like to come to the museum to see some other examples of Eerie Script. And I'm sure I can find some fruitcake."

"Thanks, but we can't," says Violet quickly. "We're going to the book dispensary. Jenny will be worrying about me, and Herbie needs to consult the mermonkey. Don't you, Herbie?"

Do I? I glare at Violet. I've no intention of doing any such thing, but before I can say so, Violet winks. And then I understand that making this excuse at least means that we can escape from the doctor. Annoyingly, though, the doc replies, "Then allow me to escort you. The streets are difficult to navigate with all the storm damage, and it's the least I can do to see you safely home, Violet."

The doc is right about one thing: the narrow streets of Eerie are in a terrible state. All around us people are still boarding up broken windows and sweeping smashed roof tiles. Some of the buildings have alarming cracks in them.

We come out into the square called Fargazi Round and pass in front of Mrs Fossil's Flotsamporium. Normally, on the pavement outside the beachcombing shop there are baskets of driftwood sticks, fossils by the nodule and crafty knick-knacks made of tide-twisted plastic. Even the letters of FLOTSAMPORIUM are made from twists of rope, sea-bent spoons and rock-chewed Frisbees and flip-flops. But today the pavement is bare, and the sign is missing a letter or two.

The doc tries to hurry us past, but the unmistakable face of Mrs Fossil appears in the glass of the peeling shop door. In a moment the door is flung open.

"Hello, my dears!" she calls, beaming her snaggletooth grin. She's wearing a lumpy knitted pullover and, for once, not a single hat. "Where are you going, I wonder?" She peers suspiciously at Dr Thalassi. "Would you like to pop in for tea and something nice? I've been baking."

"We can't, thanks," says Violet. "We need to get to the book dispensary."

"But you're soaked through!" Mrs F looks at our clothes, which are still soggy from the boat trip. "You should dry out by my stove, or you'll catch your deaths of cold."

"In point of fact," the doc states, with a cool look at the beachcomber, "it is not possible to catch a cold simply by being out in the wet, Mrs Fossil. Let alone a 'death'. A cold is a viral infection."

"Oh, well, I won't argue with a man of science, I'm sure," Mrs F sniffs. "Even if all I'm trying to do is look after these young people."

"I am already looking after them," the doc scowls in reply. "And I will make sure that they dry out as soon as we reach the bookshop."

"Then I'd better come along too," Mrs F shoots back at him. "Hold on, I'll just grab my basket."

And before anyone can think how to stop her, Mrs Fossil joins us, a large basket under one arm, covered over with a tartan tea towel.

"So, Herbie," she says, edging in front of Dr Thalassi as the four of us walk on, "have you had a chance to think more about my lovely fish-shaped bottle? I don't want to assume anything, I'm sure, but I *have* cleared a nice space in my shop window, and got some fairy lights ready—"

"In the castle," the doc booms, trying to step back in front of the beachcomber, "I have a magnificent first-century Roman pillar on which to display the bottle. It will have pride of place in the museum entranceway—"

"No, it will not!" cries Mrs Fossil.

"But my museum is so much more suitable than your … your…" Dr Thalassi struggles to finish the sentence.

Mrs Fossil comes to a halt and squares up to the doctor.

"My *what*?"

"Your *bric-a-brac* shop."

"Bric-a-brac!" Mrs F splutters. "Oh, but of course, the 'great curator' thinks his crummy old museum is *so* superior…"

"Stop!" cries Violet. "Are you two really going to do this?"

"Do what?" say Mrs Fossil and the doc together.

"Fall out over a stupid fish-shaped bottle."

The two adults glare at each other. Then Mrs Fossil sighs.

"No, no." She lets a wary smile twitch across her face, and darts a look at the curator. "No, we're not really falling out, are we, Doc? I mean, not *really*?"

The doc glares at the beachcomber as if he is about to launch a devastating reply and blast her to bits. But then the furious look evaporates, and he lowers his eyes in embarrassment. He pokes a piece of broken tile with the tip of one of his patent leather shoes.

"No, indeed not," he says with a sheepish grin. "I apologize, Wendy, for any rudeness."

"I apologize too," Mrs Fossil says. "I don't know what came over me."

But I think I do. That bottle is dividing the town – and it's starting to feel as though I can't walk anywhere without being pestered about it!

If Violet had hoped confronting the two adults would shame them into leaving us alone, she must be disappointed. They remain with us as we enter Dolphin Square, pass the bronze statue in the centre that gives it its name and cross the cobbles to our destination. And then there we are, the four of us, standing outside the window of the strangest bookshop in Eerie-on-Sea.

I look up into that window. Behind the glass, a ghastly simian face leers down at us over the back of an old-fashioned typewriter. In one hand, the monstrosity holds out a battered old top hat for an offering, while the other hand is clutched crookedly to its breast. Its lower end is an iridescent fish tail, curling around a circus pedestal of flaky red and gold.

The mermonkey.

And it seems to be grinning right at me.

MYSTERIES AND MUFFINS

THE SHOP DOOR GOES *DING*, and we find ourselves in the tall, book-lined interior that has become Violet's home. The owner of the shop, Jenny Hanniver, is stoking a blazing fire in the black marble fireplace – the smell of woodsmoke mixing with the heady scent of thousands upon thousands of books.

"Violet!" Jenny drops the poker in the log basket and comes over to hug her. "I've been worried!"

Since Vi came to live permanently in Eerie-on-Sea, Jenny – with her long red curls and green patterned shawl – is the nearest thing Violet has to a guardian.

"I'm sorry, Jenny," says Violet, from inside the shawl. Then she steps back and adds, "Has there been…?"

But Jenny shakes her head.

"No," she says. "I'm sorry. No letters, no news. But never give up hope, Violet. Your parents will find their way home to you some day…"

… *if they possibly can.*

This last bit wasn't said out loud, but I think we all know that Jenny was thinking it. Violet's parents haven't been seen since she was a baby, but she has reasons to think they are out there somewhere, searching for her. It's not for Jenny or me or anyone else to tell her otherwise.

"I heard you stayed with Herbie last night." Jenny puts on a brisk smile as she changes the subject. "Because of the storm."

I'm about to wonder how she heard this when there's a purr. Erwin slinks into the room and coils himself around Violet's legs.

"Hey there, moggy." I rumple the cat's head, feeling a bit bad when I see his cut whiskers. "Thanks for helping us earlier."

Erwin bites my hand.

It's not a real "Argh, die, human!" bite, more of an "I've nearly forgiven you, but not quite" nip. Pretty standard for the Eerie Book Dispensary's cat, though I'm left rubbing my hand all the same.

"I was just starting to wonder if I should advertise for a new assistant," Jenny says to Violet. Then she looks at the rest of us. "And now here you are with a whole troop of customers."

"I was just passing by," explains the doc, "and it seemed to me that our young friends here needed a little help…"

"And I saw them passing by," Mrs Fossil chimes in, "while I was waiting for my freshly baked salty caramel muffins to cool…"

"Salty caramel muffins!" I gasp in dreamy delight, and then blush as everyone turns to look at me. Oops, did I say that out loud?

"Still warm, too," Mrs Fossil says, her face beaming as she lifts the tea towel. Instantly, the scrummy smell of sponge cake and caramel bursts from the basket and makes my mind roll over like a puppy. "They're, um, they're your favourites, aren't they, Herbie?"

Dr Thalassi scowls as he drapes his coat over a chair and holds his hands to the fire.

"Herbie's favourite muffins?" he says, narrowing his eyes at the beachcomber. "How considerate of you to have baked those."

"Well, I just thought it was time we made a bit more

fuss of our favourite Lost-and-Founder." Mrs Fossil offers the basket to me. The little caramel chunks that burst through the sugar-crusted tops of the muffins are half melted, just the way I like them. "I was going to drop them off at the hotel later today, Herbie. But, well, since we're all here…"

It's probably a bit rude of me to just reach out and take a muffin, but I can't help it. I have the thing hot and squidgy in my hand when Dr Thalassi speaks again.

"You know, Herbie," he says, "I was thinking of popping around too. I wondered if we should restart your lessons. It's been a while since you last came to class in my museum, but I promised I'd take care of your schooling when you first arrived in town, and I'm ashamed to say that I've let that promise slide. How would you like to come regularly and study mechanics with me again?"

"Really?" I say, pausing with the muffin halfway to my mouth.

"Indeed," says the doc with a twinkle. "And it's only right that I extend the same offer to Miss Parma, now that she has come to live with us. Violet, you already come to the museum at all hours to ask about our local wildlife. How would you like to have regular classes in natural history? You and Herbie could come together."

I lower the muffin from my open mouth and turn to look at Vi. My mind fills with a happy memory of cluttered desks and fine-quality tools, and the doc explaining the workings of levers and gears. I hadn't realized how much I missed those days, but I do! I owe almost everything I know about fixing things to Dr Thalassi. I'd love to learn more – to sit with Violet in the comfort of Dr T's fabulous study, uncovering the mysteries of the universe together...

"Muffins!" Mrs Fossil shouts, waking me from my daydream. "Hundreds of muffins! To help you study!"

"Oh, stop!" cries Violet. "This is ridiculous."

Muffins are never ridiculous, I almost say, but I'm glad I don't, because Violet looks serious.

"Can't you hear yourselves?" she goes on, looking at each of the adults in turn. "Now you're trying to *bribe* Herbie. It's already hard enough for him to know what to do with that bottle, without all this."

I take a bite from the muffin. It's yummy, but I feel as though it would have been even yummier a moment ago.

"This wouldn't be the fish-shaped bottle everyone is talking about, would it?" says Jenny.

"Everyone?" My heart sinks.

"These things get around, Herbie." Jenny nods. "And the townsfolk are very nervous. The storm has done a lot of damage, and this is a strange time for anything connected to the legend of Saint Dismal to come to light. So, was there anything inside this bottle?"

Everyone turns to look at me.

"I'm, um, I'm keeping the whole business under my hat," I say, with a glance at Violet. "Till I can work out what to do about it."

"I see," says Jenny, glancing briefly at my Lost-and-Founder's cap and then searching my eyes. "Well, in the meantime, why don't you pull up a chair while I put the kettle on. And then perhaps we can *all* have a muffin."

And with that, she heads to the door behind the shop counter marked PRIVATE. But she stops halfway through.

"You know, Herbie, if you're really stuck working out what to do, maybe the mermonkey can help."

MAMMOTHS AND
NARWHALS

"HOW IS BLAZE WESTERLEY?" Dr Thalassi asks,
once we're all around the fire and Jenny has brought tea
and plates. "Poor boy. I tried to visit him after his uncle
drowned, but Boadicea Bates said the fisherfolk look after
their own. I hope that's true, because Blaze will be all
alone in the world now – and barely sixteen years old."

"I think he's doing OK, considering," says Vi. Then
she reaches to her coat – hanging to dry by the fire –
and pulls the large sheet of folded paper from the inside
pocket. She opens it out fully on the floor in front of us.

"I made a copy of the secret writing on the sides of
the bottle," she says to the doc. "What can you tell me
about it?

"Ah, yes, the Eerie Script," says the doc, allowing his

spectacles to fall onto the bridge of his nose. "But I don't remember there being quite so much of it on the bottle. Where did you find these other examples?"

Beside the rubbing are several small lines of the mysterious runes, in Violet's handwriting.

"I copied them," says Violet, "from a chart in Blaze's boat, a chart that belonged to Squint Westerley. I think Blaze's uncle knew how to read and write Eerie Script. Is that possible, Doctor?"

"Hardly!" says the doc, with a snort of disbelief. "It's an ancient form of writing whose secret has been lost to history. No one has been able to read and write Eerie Script for centuries."

"No one at all?"

The doc smiles an indulgent smile. "I have devoted a great deal of time to the problem myself, Violet. As I said, we have examples in the museum. But there aren't enough to make a proper analysis."

"Analysis?" I say. "What do you mean?"

"Well, if each of these marks is a letter, then we can compare how often they appear in different inscriptions. For example, the letter 'E' is the most commonly used letter in our language. So, if we can find the most common symbol, we can guess that it stands for 'E'. In this way, we could at least determine if the language encoded is our own, and not some other language written in a strange alphabet. But as you can see from these examples, the symbols differ slightly from inscription to inscription."

"Except for the crosses," says Vi. "Every inscription starts and ends with a cross, like this." And she points to an example:

$$\dagger \ \curlyvee \nearrow \mid \mathcal{V} \nearrow \mid \mid \uparrow \cdot \mid \mid \mid \mathcal{V} \uparrow \cdot \mid \mid \mathcal{L} \ \mathcal{V} \mathcal{K} \uparrow \cdot \mid \mathcal{V} \mathcal{V}$$
$$\uparrow \cdot \mid \mid \mathcal{L} \ \mathcal{V} \mathcal{K} \uparrow \mid \mathcal{V} \mathcal{V} \mid \cdot \mid \mid \mathcal{V} \mathcal{V} \ \curlyvee \nearrow \mid \mathcal{X}$$

"Indeed." Dr Thalassi blinks at Violet. "I'm impressed that you noticed."

Vi glares out from inside her hair.

"I'm trying to learn how to *read* this code, Doctor, not collecting it for fun."

"You think it *is* a code, then?" I say. "As in, each symbol stands for a letter?"

"Yes." Violet chews the end of her pen. "I do now. Though that doesn't explain why the shapes differ slightly in each message. Something else must be going on."

"I would advise you to abandon this, Violet." The doc's eyebrows lower into a single caterpillar of discouragement. "The problem is very difficult, and…"

But Violet doesn't seem to be listening.

"Perhaps if we look at them in a mirror…" she says, snatching a shiny cake knife from a nearby plate and licking the crumbs off. She holds the reflective surface up to the peculiar runes, one by one. When that doesn't satisfy her, she says, "Or maybe it's mathematical. Maybe these dots correspond to numbers somehow…"

Then, as if she has forgotten that the rest of us are here, Vi takes her pen and crawls across the paper spread over the floor, scribbling notes and sums and talking to herself.

"Golly!" says Mrs Fossil.

"That's a dead end too." Dr Thalassi gently removes the pen from Violet's hand, just as she's about to write on his shoe. "I have already investigated the mathematical route. I urge you, Violet, to spare yourself a good deal of frustration and give this up. I admire your determination, but you are not likely to succeed where many others have tried and failed. Besides, writing on the floor will give you a bad back."

"Just because you gave up –" Violet sits up and folds her arms – "doesn't mean I should too."

"I didn't give up, Violet. I simply haven't succeeded yet." Dr Thalassi hands back her pen. "When you come for those lessons, we can discuss the matter further."

At this, Violet looks a bit less annoyed. She takes a muffin of her own and sits in the middle of her paper to eat it.

"Doc," I say, "did you know that Squint Westerley was building an electric engine for his boat?"

"I did. Though he was very secretive about it. I offered to advise him, but he refused. I fear he never quite forgave me for that tusk business."

"Tusk business?"

"Yes," says the doc, taking a cup of tea from Jenny and politely refusing milk. "I expect you noticed it on the prow of his boat. It was the tusk he brought back after his lucky escape from drowning, all those years ago. He made extraordinary claims about it. He said it belonged to a gigantic creature he saw at the bottom of the sea."

"Gigantic?" Violet says. "Or *Gar*gantic?"

"The fishermen might agree with you, Violet," the doc replies with a chuckle. "They are extremely superstitious. Anyway, when Squint brought the object to me for identification, I was able to tell him it was merely the tusk of an extinct woolly mammoth. They sometimes wash up on the coast here, and his was a finely preserved example. A little straight, perhaps, and rather overlong, but almost certainly *Mammuthus primigenius* – a species from the late Pleistocene."

"*Almost* certainly?" I say. "So you're not really sure?"

"Hmm," the doc replies. "Anyway, looking back, I should perhaps have told Squint Westerley this in private. Telling him in front of the other fishermen made his life quite difficult. They laughed at him all the more after that."

"Doc!" Mrs Fossil looks shocked. "You didn't ought to have done that. Mind you, when he asked me what I thought it was, I said it was probably a narwhal tooth. You know, a 'sea unicorn', as some call them? But at least I told him that on the quiet. And at least I said 'probably' – you can get out of a load of trouble by using a word like 'probably'."

"The blame isn't all mine." The doc sips his tea. "He asked others, too. I believe he even took it to Sebastian Eels."

At the mention of Sebastian Eels, Violet puts her muffin down, half eaten. Her father's arch-enemy may be dead and gone, but his name still has the power to put her off even Mrs Fossil's baking. And as the author of *The Cold, Dark Bottom of the Sea*, he's not my favourite person either. I glance over my shoulder and see the hairy back of the mermonkey, hunched as if challenging me to approach.

"That rotter!" says Mrs F. "What did *he* say Squint's tusk was, I wonder?"

Dr Thalassi pulls a disapproving face. No one liked Sebastian Eels much.

"Goodness only knows. But few people knew our Eerie legends and folklore like Eels did. I remember he took the tusk away for several weeks, to examine it."

"Poor old Squint." Mrs Fossil shakes her head. "He never did recover from that whole sorry episode. The other fishermen teased him cruelly."

"True," agrees the doc. "But what any of it means is anyone's guess. Neither Sebastian Eels nor Squint Westerley is alive to tell us, so I doubt we'll ever know. And I don't see how any of this can be connected to our current storm…"

But the doc's words die away as the Eerie Book Dispensary starts to shake.

STORMQUAKE!

FIRST THE CUPS START TO JANGLE, the tea inside them rippling like the surfaces of miniature seas. Then Mrs Fossil's basket falls off the arm of her chair as the rumbling increases.

"Heavens alive!" Jenny cries as all around us books begin to dance on their shelves, shrugging out of their places and flapping open as they topple to the ground. Over us, in the midnight blue of the ceiling, white cracks appear and showers of plaster rain down, covering us with a fine powder.

The mermonkey's head wobbles eerily, and its hat falls to the floor in a cloud of dust.

Then the shaking ends.

"Not again!" Mrs Fossil clutches the arms of her chair. "Another stormquake!"

"*Earth*quake, more like it," says the doc, jumping to his feet and grabbing his coat and hat. "The storm is still far out over the bay."

"But since when do we have earthquakes in Eerie-on-Sea?"

"Since the storm blew up, that's when." Jenny looks around in dismay at the books covering the floor. "And they're getting worse."

"Gargantis wakes, Eerie quakes," says Violet.

"I must go back to the museum and check my seismographs," Dr Thalassi declares, ignoring Violet and heading to the door. "If the tremors worsen, we might have to consider evacuating the town."

"What?" cries Mrs Fossil. "Wait for me, Doc. I need to check up on my Flotsamporium."

And with that, they both leave, Mrs Fossil snatching up her basket as she goes.

Jenny fetches a dustpan and brush, while Violet starts to gather up books. I pick up the spilled muffins and wish that there was some way to remove plaster from salty caramel.

"Wiaow," says a voice, and I see that Erwin has the mermonkey's top hat in his teeth. I stoop and pick up the hat, dusting it off with my cuff.

"Thanks, puss," I say, and go to replace the top hat back in the mermonkey's crooked paw. The creature leers down at me, waiting. Even though its light-bulb eyes are not lit up, there seems to be a twinkle in them.

I freeze.

The mermonkey is activated by a coin thrown in the hat, but as Jenny always says, sometimes you don't even need to do that. Some people have only to touch the hat in the creature's hand to set off the mechanism and be dispensed a book.

I slowly move my hand away, still holding the top hat.

I notice Violet watching me from behind a pile of books in her arms.

"Nice try," I snap to the cat.

Erwin gives a twitch of irritation, then turns his bottom towards me in disgust.

"But why not, Herbie?" says Violet. "What are you scared of?"

I stare at the hat and think about *The Cold, Dark Bottom of the Sea* by Sebastian Eels. Could I have been wrong about it being a warning, after all? A warning to never go to sea again? If I *am* wrong, then think of all the books I've missed by never consulting the mermonkey again! And yet, when it comes to the mystery of my origins, and the fate of my family, being given a book about a shipwreck is surely more than coincidence. It's easier for Violet. She thinks she might see her parents again. What if a new book just confirms the fact that I don't even have that slim hope?

"A book is like a mirror," says a feline voice. "We always see ourselves inside."

Erwin has climbed up into a gap in a bookshelf and is giving me the frosty eye.

I stick my tongue out at him. Well, he deserves it for interfering. Then I drop the hat onto a nearby chair and shove my hands in my pockets.

I won't be consulting the mermonkey today, or any other day, and that's flat.

"Oh, Herbie!" Violet puts the books down, snatches up the hat and then wedges it roughly between the fingers of the mermonkey's extended hand. The creature trembles on its pedestal, but it remains inactive.

"There!" she says to me. "Happy now?"

I consider sticking my tongue out at Violet, too, but before I can, she speaks again.

"Toss me a coin," she says. "From the jar behind the counter. I'm going to show you it's OK, by getting a book for myself."

I tip a coin out of the jar – a nice shiny one – and flick it over to Violet.

The coin flashes silver as it flies between us. But instead of catching it, Violet steps to one side, and with a deft movement, she nudges the coin with her elbow...

... straight into the mermonkey's hat.

The creature's eyes light up, and it begins to scream.

"That's not fair!" I cry over the mechanical shrieks of the creature. Already it has raised its hat with a creaking, clanking sound and plopped it on its head. The coin clatters down into the mechanism.

"It's completely fair," Violet calls back. "This way, whatever book comes out, it will have been chosen for *us both*."

By now the mermonkey's eyes have lit up and puffs of smoke wreathe its head, filling the room with a familiar pong – a pong, if you are wondering, that is a mix of burnt fur, overheated electric wires and the metallic, oily tang of a creaky old clockwork machine on its last gasp. If Eerie-on-Sea ever produced a perfume, it'd smell something like this, and no one would buy it.

The mermonkey uncurls its arm over the typewriter keys, extends one bony index finger, and – with a violent jabbing motion – begins to type.

Klack, klack, klickety-klack.

Then, as suddenly as it began, it stops. Its hand retracts, its eye lights flicker out, and the mechanism judders to a halt.

There's a *ping!* and a postcard is projected from the typewriter. It spins away in an arc, circles the book-lined room and boomerangs back to land at my feet.

With a shaking hand, I pick up the card.

On one side is the usual printed drawing of the mermonkey, but on the other is the important bit – a series of letters and numbers that looks like this:

2 - 3 - N - Mb - 54

It appears as though I've consulted the mermonkey after all.

CLARITY MARKS

THERE AREN'T MANY PEOPLE who know how to read the mermonkey's book code, though *you* might, if you've been to Eerie-on-Sea before. The machine made such an impression on me when I first consulted it that *I've* never been able to forget.

2 - 3 - N - Mb - 54

2: This number represents the floor of the shop your book is located on. In other words, the book is upstairs on the second floor.

3: This is the room on the second floor we need to go to. In this case, the third room. I say "we", but I've decided that I don't want anything to do with this book. Violet's gone without me, and if you listen carefully, you can still hear her footsteps as she runs up the wooden staircase.

N: Now, this letter indicates which wall of the third room the book is on. 'N', of course, means the north wall. It's easy to orientate yourself when you live by the sea, and Violet knows it all by heart anyway.

Mb: OK, here's where it gets a bit tricky. All the shelves in the book dispensary are painted in different colours, but it's the *same order* of colours on every wall. The topmost shelf is always painted midnight blue – or "Mb", as the mermonkey types it – to match the ceiling. And that faint creaking sound we can hear? Well, that'll be Violet clipping the tall bamboo ladder to the ceiling rail so she can climb.

She'll be up there now, teetering on the top, counting along the spines on the shelf until she gets to fifty-four. And if there aren't fifty-four books on the shelf? Well, she'll just have to start counting back when she reaches the end, won't she?

There's a bang from upstairs as Violet slides back down the ladder.

"Did I hear the mermonkey?" says Jenny, reappearing with a broom and dustpan.

"Violet did it," I reply in a sulk. "It's nothing to do with me. She'll be down in a moment with some cheery book about being brave and facing up to your fears,

I expect. Then we'll head off with a spring in her step, while she tells me that she was right all along and I'm just a chump. Look, here she comes now."

And it's true. Violet walks into the room with her hands behind her back.

But there's no spring in her step. She looks troubled.

"Violet, what's wrong?" says Jenny.

"We need to go," Violet replies, avoiding my eye. She picks up her coat and slips something into her pocket. That something, of course, is a book.

"Vi?" I feel a coldness grip my stomach. "What is it? What book did you get?"

"I didn't," she says, pulling her coat on. "I, um, I think you did."

"But you said it was being chosen for both of us!"

"Who touched the coin?" asks Jenny.

Violet continues to avoid my gaze. The coin only bounced off her pullover. *I* was the last one to actually touch it.

And the card landed at *my* feet.

"But it can't be *that* bad, surely?" says Jenny, looking between us both.

"Violet!" I cry.

Finally, she looks up.

So I do the eyebrow at her.

I don't often get to do the eyebrow – it's normally other people doing it to me – but for once it's my turn. I do the eyebrow, and the eyebrow says it all.

Violet sighs.

"All right," she says. "Just promise you won't freak out, Herbie, OK?"

I give out a squeak that I couldn't suppress even if my life depended on it.

"Hey, it's all right," says Jenny, coming over and putting her arm around my shoulders. "Books are nothing to be scared of. Why are you worried, Herbie?"

"Herbie never consults the mermonkey," says Vi. "Ever."

"Yes, he does." Jenny laughs as she replies. "He did so when he first arrived, though I remember he tried to keep that book secret. And then ... now, let me see ... um, well, there was that time when..."

She looks at me.

"But, Herbie, you're here all the time. Are you saying you *never* get dispensed a book?"

"Not after that first time, no." I glare at Violet. "Until now."

Jenny holds her hand out.

"Come on," she says to Vi. "Give it to me. *Not*

showing him is even worse."

Violet slips the book out of her pocket and hands it to Jenny, who holds it up to look. I can see from the back that it's a clothbound hardback in blue. A deep, dark, under-the-sea type of blue.

"*Set Course for the Storm,*" Jenny reads the title aloud, "by Clarity Marks. I don't see why that's so troubling. It's a good book, actually. It's the true account of an explorer who survived terrible weather by navigating straight through it. She wrote this book herself. Here, Herbie, you might enjoy it."

She passes me the book.

And Jenny might be right, if there was nothing but the title and the author's name on the cover.

But there's also an illustration – a picture of a small sailing boat on the crest of a monster wave, its sails torn to shreds. The boat looks as if it's about to be smashed to matchwood by a storm that rages above it, as a single human figure clings on for dear life. And below the heaving waterline, twisting and turning around the author's name, is a long, sinuous tentacle, snaking up from the depths of the ocean to seize the boat. Snaking up, that is, from the cold, dark bottom of the sea.

DIAMOND-SHAPED PANES

"HERBIE, WAIT!"

I'm running, which is why Violet has to shout this. And as I had a head start – out of the book dispensary like a shot – Violet's struggling to catch up.

I race down the street, jumping and weaving around people repairing their storm-damaged property, heaping sandbags against doors and preparing for the return of the storm.

And where am I running to?

Well, see for yourself. I jump the last few steps into Tenby Twist and skid to a halt in the grubby shadows at the back of an old half-timbered building. As I struggle to get my breath back, Violet catches up, also breathing heavily.

"Herbie!" she gasps. "What ... are you doing? What is this place?"

"Pub," I manage to say, pointing to where the sign of the Whelk & Walrus swings with a gibbet creak. A strong whiff of pipe tobacco, greasy food and damp waterproofs fills the air. From inside the building can be heard the lusty sound of a sea shanty being sung by a large group of men.

"Pub?"

"Fishermen," I explain, pulling the front of my uniform flat as I get my breath back. "I've come to see Boadicea Bates and her crew."

"What?"

"It turns out you were right," I explain. "The mer-monkey *has* helped me decide what to do with the fish-shaped bottle. Or, at least, what I should do with this."

And I pull my cap from my head.

Freed from confinement, the little crackling light – the sprightning, as we now know it's called – crawls sleepily out from within my mad, sherbety locks and takes to the air. In a moment, it's fluttering about over my head on tiny electrical wings, chasing the dingy shadows from behind the pub with its wondrous light.

"Herbie, they'll see!" Vi hisses, grabbing my hat and trying to cover up the sprightning again.

"I want them to," I reply, reaching up and catching the little creature in my hands.

"It's never been about the bottle, Vi," I say. "It's what was in the bottle that matters."

And I open my hands. The little creature fizzes and crackles where she sits in my palm.

"Mrs Fossil and the doc will have to find a way to share the bottle itself," I continue. "It's only mouldy old glass, anyway. I'm giving the sprightning to Boadicea."

"But *why*?"

"Because I'm a Lost-and-Founder, Vi, not a zookeeper for magical creatures! Because the mermonkey is *still* warning me about boats. Because Deep Hood terrifies me, and he wants this sprightning thing. So I say let him fight Boadicea for it. I don't see why any of this should have anything to do with me."

Vi looks cross. "But you were entrusted with it. *You*, Herbie! Surely there's a rule of lost-and-foundering that means you can't just give up. And what would Boadicea Bates do to this poor little creature? What would Deep Hood do to her?"

I look down into my hands. The sprightning

sparkles. In the dazzle I can't see a face, but somehow I know she's gazing up at me.

Why did Violet have to mention the rules of lost-and-foundering?

Because, of course, she's right.

I throw up my hands and propel the little electrical fairy into the air. Maybe, after all this, she'll just fly away. But she doesn't. She turns one fluttering orbit of my head before coming to hover over it again, making my scalp tingle with static. Then she lands and crawls back into my hair.

With a sigh, I jam the cap back on my head and the light is hidden once more.

"Thank you!" says Violet, clearly relieved. Then she glances at a nearby window. "And now, since we're here, let's take a look at what the fishermen are up to."

We press our faces to the tiny diamond-shaped panes of glass. Inside the pub, in a golden fug of steamy air and smoke, is a large group of fishermen, drinking pints of beer and talking in low voices.

"I can't hear anything," Vi whispers. "Can you?"

I'm just about to suggest trying a different window when we see, through the smoke and vapour, a rectangle of light as the front door of the pub swings open. The

fishermen go quiet as a tall and terrible figure enters the
Whelk & Walrus.

Deep Hood has arrived.

DRASTIC ACTION

THE WHELK & WALRUS PUB is not like this in the summer.

When the tourists are here, the fishermen keep away, and the landlord scrubs the place down. He puts out a sign saying FAMILIES WELCOME and sets little tables and chairs on the quayside, with a quirky "seaside" menu and candles in the evening. Out-of-towners nibble crab sandwiches and speciality ice cream in crispy cones as they coo over the quaint doings of the fisherfolk out on the harbour wall. Some nights there's even a quiz.

No true fisherman of Eerie would be seen dead in the place then.

But the world turns and the season ends and the out-of-towners drift away. The last tourists to retreat from the Whelk & Walrus are driven from it by a rising tide of sullen knitwear and heavy beards as the nights draw in and the fisherfolk return. Pipes are smoked once more as sea songs are sung and beer is spilled and fights erupt, and Boadicea Bates presides over it all.

In the winter months, families are most definitely *not* welcome in the Whelk & Walrus Pub.

"We should go, Vi," I whisper, feeling sick at the sight of Deep Hood.

But Violet ignores me. She remains at the window, watching.

Inside, Deep Hood crashes his metal-bound box onto a table and sits beside the roaring fire. The fishermen hang back, but Boadicea Bates steps forward. She speaks, but we can't hear what she's saying. After a moment, the hood twitches as Deep Hood begins a reply.

Violet whispers something that sounds like, *We need to get inside, Herbie,* but since that would be bonkers, I must be mistaken. Then she leans over and says it again, this time straight into my ear.

"We need to get inside, Herbie. We can't hear anything out here."

I blink at her.

"We can't go in there *now*."

"We have to," Violet says. "Something tells me that what's being said in there is important. Besides, you wanted to go in a moment ago."

"That was before Deep Hood showed up!" I hiss, but Violet has already crept around to the back of the pub.

The alley behind the Whelk & Walrus is filthy and chaotic and stinks of spilled dustbins and dead fish. Last night's storm has only made this worse. Violet picks her way over to the back door of the pub and tests it.

It's unlocked.

Before I can say anything, she ducks inside. Then she peeks back out and beckons to me.

"Violet!" I whisper-shout, joining her at the door. "We can't just—"

But she pulls me in and shuts the door, so it seems we can.

We're in a corridor, behind the bar. Through a doorway inside, the steady drone of voices can be heard, and the bristly back of a barman's neck can be seen as he pulls a pint. Violet puts her finger to her lips and very carefully removes a long, waxed hooded coat – which is wet, and probably belongs to one of the fishermen – from a peg. She slips it on, then takes down another and hands it to me.

I pull the coat on over my uniform. The hood engulfs me with darkness and the smell of engine grease and industrial-strength skin cream. But at least it will hide my Lost-and-Founder's cap.

"I can't believe we're doing this," I whisper, making Violet put an urgent finger back to her lips. The barman twitches and glances back in our direction. We shrink into the shadows, straining to hear what's being said, but still the voices are just a hum of sound.

Violet points into a second corridor, and we tiptoe along it, passing a small drippy room that smells so horrible it can only be the pub toilets. We hurry past and climb a short flight of stairs. At the top of the stairs is a door, and on the door is a greasy sign:

ᕤBALCONYᕤ

I feel like I've been tipped into a nightmare as I see Violet reach out a hand, push the door open, and slip inside.

We find ourselves in a gloomy space overlooking the crowded main room of the pub. There's a staircase of treacly wood that leads down to the bar, but I'm relieved to see there's no one up here on the balcony right now. We slip into chairs at a table beside the balustrade, which gives us a great view down on the bar room below. And if anyone looks up? Well, in the dark, smoky air – and dressed in our borrowed fisherman's coats and hoods – we shouldn't be noticed. I flash Violet a "I hope you know what you're doing" look, and she gives me an encouraging grin. Then we look down into the bar, where Deep Hood is speaking again.

"It is time," he drawls in his careful, slippery voice, "to take drastic action."

"Aye," says Boadicea Bates, who is standing in the centre of the room, though not too close to Deep Hood. "We cannot allow this Lost-and-Founder – this *boy* – to stand in our way, can we, lads?"

There is a chorus of snarled agreement from the other fishermen.

"I don't suppose," says Deep Hood, once this has died down, "anyone would notice if Herbert Lemon met with a little accident. The storm is returning, fiercer than ever. People would think he got swept off the harbour wall and washed out to sea."

There's another rumble of agreement at this, but it

sounds a bit less certain than before. The fishermen all look at one another.

"Wouldn't that be ...?" says one.

"... a bit *too* drastic?" says another.

Deep Hood lifts his metal box and bangs it down on the table with a *CRASH!*

The fishermen jump.

"Are these hard men of the sea I hear speaking?" gurgles Deep Hood. "What would your ancestors say if they could see you standing here in doubt? Or are the fisherfolk of Eerie now so soft that they can't do what needs to be done?"

There's an angry growl of annoyance around the room.

"We ARE men of the sea!" one man shouts.

And another adds, "Aye, we could do it."

"It's just ..." says another, "the Lost-and-Founder is only a boy."

"Aye," says a fisherman with a lanky beard. "I was there when he was found, washed up on the beach in a crate of lemons. Just a weedy child."

"But he is not –" Deep Hood rises to his feet – "a child of Eerie! What do you, the heirs of Saint Dismal, the fisherfolk of Eerie-on-Sea, care about an outsider?"

"Very well," declares Boadicea Bates, "to destroy Gargantis and save the town, the boy could be sacrificed."

"Good," burbles Deep Hood. "I'm pleased that one among you, at least, has the will to do what must be done."

Deep Hood starts to lower himself back into his seat, but before he gets there, the fisherman with the lanky beard speaks up again.

"What about you, though?"

A silence follows this. Everyone turns to look at Lanky Beard. The fisherman goes a bit pale and clearly wishes he hadn't spoken at all, but he ploughs on.

"I mean, you're a stranger and all. That's to say, you're not from around these parts neither. We've never even seen your face. And now *you're* telling us what we should and shouldn't do—"

Before Lanky Beard can finish, Deep Hood's hood trembles, and the pink whippy thing we saw back on the boat shoots out and strikes Lanky Beard in the face. The fisherman staggers back, clutching at his eyes, but the thing darts at him again, this time grabbing his beard and yanking his head down onto a tabletop. The fisherman reels away in shock, before the pink whip darts out a third time, punching the man's feet out from under him. He goes down with a sickening crunch, and stays down.

And then we finally get a good look at this fearsome weapon and realize with horror that our first impression – the one we had back on the *Jornty Spark* – was right after all.

"It *is* a tentacle!" Violet whispers to me, clutching at my arm.

As we watch, mesmerized, the pink and repulsive tentacle, with gaping suckers along its underside, coils in languid triumph over the crumpled body of the sailor. Then it retracts into Deep Hood's hood, with a disgusting smacking sound.

"Do not dare to question me!" gurgles Deep Hood in his slippery voice. "There is more Eerie in my blood than you could possibly imagine."

Another silence follows this. There's a moment before it's broken by the tremulous but determined voice of Boadicea Bates.

"Now now, th-there's no need to be hasty, sir. Scaring's one thing, but killing? Well, that's a hard business, that is. 'Specially when it's just a child. But I said we could do it, and we will. It's just … might there yet be another way?"

Deep Hood lets out a watery hiss of menace.

"Maybe you won't be so soft when you hear what this Lemon child has done."

"Done?"

"Yes, Boadicea Bates. This child you are being so precious about has done something unforgivable. He has opened the bottle. Herbert Lemon has opened the fish-shaped bottle, and he has *taken what's inside!*"

CLAMMY DODGER

THE ROAR OF FURY that meets Deep Hood's words is louder than thunder. The fishermen stamp their feet and wave their fists in the air, and my insides turn to ice as I sit up on the balcony and realize that all this fury is being directed at me! I feel a tingling as the sprightning starts getting agitated. I give my widest of wide-eyed looks at Vi and hope she thinks we've heard enough now.

Violet looks shocked, but she doesn't get up. Down below, the anger subsides, and it's clear that Violet is determined to witness what happens next.

"How do you know this?" demands Boadicea Bates. "How do you know the boy has opened the bottle and stolen the light?"

Deep Hood, still standing beside the fireplace, raises one arm and presents his gloved hand, palm upwards, to Boadicea Bates. She takes a step back.

"I have," he says, "my spies."

Something moves in Deep Hood's drooping sleeve. For a moment it seems as if the tentacle might reappear, but then I let out a gasp of surprise.

The clockwork hermit crab emerges from the sleeve.

It does so slowly, as if assessing its surroundings, reaching with one cautious brass leg and then another, before climbing onto the man's outstretched hand. Its iridescent shell and gleaming workmanship are so fine that it seems entirely out of place in this dreary place, and in such sinister company.

"*This* is your spy?" says Boadicea, amazed.

"My spy, and my slave," declares Deep Hood, tipping his hand. The hermit crab is suddenly falling. It twists in the air, extending its sword arms with a *schlaak!* to absorb the shock of landing. The shell regains its balance and then raises its swords threateningly at the fishermen in a way I know all too well. I rub the cut on the back of my hand.

"It's fixed!" I hiss to Vi, remembering how I'd repaired

one of those broken sword arms myself and left it on my desk with a replacement bolt. "Someone's been in my cellar!"

"My mechanical spy discovered the crime this morning," Deep Hood tells the room. "There is a small hole melted through the bottle's stopper. The Gargantic Light is gone."

At this, there are more cries of outrage from the fishermen.

Deep Hood stoops and beckons the shell towards him, as if he's calling a small dog over to give it a treat. The hermit crab turns to him but hangs back.

A hiss of menace ripples the edges of the hood, and the shell clatters reluctantly forward.

"This happened because my clockwork slave failed to bring me the bottle last night as I commanded," Deep Hood burbles as the shell arrives at its master's feet. "And I do not tolerate failure."

Deep Hood kicks the shell.

It's a strong, cruel kick, designed to punish.

The shell flies across the room and out of our sight. We hear it land with a *crash!* and an "OW!" from a fisherman. Someone must kick it back, because it flies into view again and lands in the middle of the bar room floor. It scrabbles back to its mechanical feet, but another fisherman steps up and kicks it too.

"Lousy thing!"

And then another.

"Stupid little spider!"

Soon the hermit crab is flying left and right, as more and more of the fishermen are drawn into the spiteful game, swearing and kicking viciously. And I feel terrible when I remember that I kicked it once too.

Overwhelmed by the fishermen, the clockwork hermit crab draws its limbs back inside its shell. When a particularly well-aimed kick sends it towards the fireplace, Deep Hood catches it out of the air, to a loud cheer from the fishermen. He shoves the shell roughly into his coat pocket and sits back down.

"At least if Herbert Lemon has the light on him," says Boadicea Bates, "it will be easy to take it. But –" and she turns to Deep Hood again – "are you sure it will lure Gargantis?"

"Still you doubt me," Deep Hood gurgles in reply. "And yet did not Saint Dismal himself lure the creature with his Gargantic Light?"

"He did!" cry the fishermen.

"And did he not preserve this miraculous light in a

bottle so that his trusted followers could use it if ever Gargantis should return?"

"He … he did?" suggests Boadicea, because now the fishermen sound less sure.

Deep Hood spits with contempt.

"It is fortunate that I am here to explain your own history to you. Have you forgotten how Saint Dismal was hailed as a hero? The saviour of the town? Have you forgotten the glory that was once his? Do you not want this for yourselves?"

"We do!" shout the fishermen, heartier than ever.

"And if it's a question of expenses…" Deep Hood adds, flipping a catch on top of his metal-bound box. The side of the box opens, and a hush falls over the room as the gleam of treasure is revealed. The box is filled with small bars of warmly glittering gold, which spill out and clatter across the tabletop.

"It *will* be an expensive business, for sure," says Boadicea after a moment, her eyes – like everyone's – fixed on the gold. "A little, er, compensation will be most welcome."

"It'll be a thirsty business, and all!" cries a fisherman, and there's a nervous laugh around the room. "I feel dry just thinking about it."

"Barman!" Deep Hood bangs the table with his fist. "Bring drinks for everyone. Tonight these brave fishermen will catch the biggest fish of their lives!"

The men cheer, and the tense atmosphere gives way to a sense of celebration. The men call for pints of Clammy Dodger, while one of them produces a squeezebox from somewhere. Music begins, and the fisherfolk break into song – a song so salty and ripe that it makes Violet's eyebrows shoot up and me blush bright red.

"Is your boat ready, Boadicea?" says Deep Hood when the music subsides.

"Aye!" declares the fisherwoman. "My fine *Bludgeon*'s shipshape and ready, and the old whaling rig is set up, as agreed. It's been a long time since we hunted something as big as a whale in these parts, but the cannon is primed, and the explosives you gave us fit beautifully on the spears. We'll bring this fish in, no matter how big it is."

"Just see that you do," replies Deep Hood. "It's no good to me on the bottom of the sea. I need it dead and beached in the harbour."

"Either way, the town will be saved…" Boadicea starts to say, but Deep Hood bangs his fist on the table again.

"I will have its carcass!" he roars. "*That* is our deal,

and you will stick to it. Any man who fails me will feel my wrath. Or any woman."

Boadicea backs away.

"But any who bring me the body of Gargantis will have their pockets filled with gold."

"We'll see it done," says Boadicea. "Won't we, lads? We need only the bait."

"Precisely," says Deep Hood. "The Gargantic Light. And the Lemon boy has it."

"Not for long!" cries a voice.

"A-ha-ha-rrr!" the men guffaw as they clash their pint glasses together, relieved to be able to pass on the threat to someone else. "We'll catch that little Lemon fish first! And that pesky book girl, too, if we have to. We'll catch everything!"

"No one fishes like an Eerie man fishes, and no one fishes like he!" sings the sailor with the squeezebox. Then the men join in, singing the next line: *"He'll catch all the day, and he'll catch all the night, and he'll* catch *all the* fish *in the* sea!"

"Rubbish!" shouts Violet in a loud voice, all roughed up to sound like a salty old sailor, and my jaw drops, because *what*? But Violet hasn't finished yet. She leans over the railing, her own hood covering her face, and calls down into the smoky bar room.

"Whatever happened to, *Be good to the sea, and she'll pay you in kind. Take just what you need, and not all that you find*?"

There's a confused rumble of responses to these words, and a few of the fishermen downstairs mutter, "Aye, 'tis true," and "It's what my grandpa always said." But I'm not really paying attention. I'm too busy shrinking down into my coat and wishing I could teleport straight to my Lost-and-Foundery. *What is Violet doing?*

"Pah!" shouts Boadicea Bates up to us. "That's all well and good, but Eerie-on-Sea is in danger. And besides, there's many here who need this gold."

There's a murmur of agreement at this, but Violet is already calling back, in her best fisherman's voice, *"By Dismal's beard! By north wind cold! We'll love the sea, and not the gold!"*

At this, the fishermen sound more uncertain than ever, and a clamour of unease rolls around the bar room below us.

"Violet!" I hiss. "Where are you getting all this stuff?"

Then I remember she's been reading a book about the old sayings of Eerie-on-Sea.

Now, I'm all for learning things from books. Really,

I am. Learning things from books is *great*! It's just that shouting those things out when you're supposed to be in disguise and not drawing attention to yourself is … well, there's probably an old saying about that too. And if there isn't, I'm going to make one up, as soon as I can think of a rhyme for *bonkers*.

"Who is that?" Boadicea calls up to us, standing in the middle of the bar room with her fists on her hips. "Is that you, Chumbly? Got a sore throat again?"

Vi sinks back from the railing. I catch a glimpse of her face in the shadows of her hood, and I suddenly understand two things: (1) even Violet thinks Violet's gone too far this time; and (2) if the fishermen don't lose interest in us, and soon, we are going to have to run very, *very* fast. The whole bar is looking up at the balcony now, and Boadicea Bates is frowning. Beside her, the dark shadow of Deep Hood's hood is turned full on us.

"Since when did Chumbly have so much hair?" says one of the fishermen.

"He doesn't," says another. "Chumbly's bald!"

Boadicea takes a step towards the balcony stairs.

"Ready?" Violet whispers to me, her eyes wide with alarm.

I nod.

And I am ready too, ready to fly like a rocket down the rear corridor and out the back door and home to the Grand Nautilus Hotel and whatever safety we can find there. And we'd probably have got a good head start, too, if what happens next didn't happen. But it does. The tentacle flies up from Deep Hood and yanks my own hood back from my head. The elastic strap holding my Lost-and-Founder's cap breaks, my hat flies off and the sprightning bursts out.

The Gargantic Light, charged up with my fear and crackling with miniature lightning, flutters over my head in full view of everyone in the Whelk & Walrus.

TOASTED
MOLLUSC

"BLADDERWRACKS!"

Violet jumps from her chair and leaps towards the back stairs – the way we came in. I grab my cap and throw off the fisherman's coat as I jump after her. There's a scrambling sound of kicked-over bar stools and angry shouts behind us, as the fishermen surge up the staircase from the bar. I run through the balcony exit with Violet, and she slams the door shut behind us.

We clatter down the rear stairs.

A fisherman staggers out of the stinking toilets in the corridor ahead of us, doing up his flies. He has a completely bald and shiny head.

"Chumbly, I presume?" I cry, barrelling past. "Coming through!"

"Oi!" the fisherman shouts. "How'd you know my name? What's going on?"

Then I hear a gasp from Violet. I turn to find that the fisherman has grabbed her.

I skid to a halt, the sprightning zooming around my head in a crazy orbit, crackling with energy.

"Is this what you're looking for?" I say, pointing to the fizzing thing.

"By Dismal's beard!" The fisherman's eyes nearly pop from his head. "The Gargantic Light!"

He lets go of Violet and swipes at the sprightning, which dodges his hand and then lets out a brilliant arc of lightning. The man is thrown off his feet as electricity scorches the mouldy wallpaper right down the corridor.

"Come on!" cries Vi.

We skid around the corner and throw ourselves at the rear door of the pub – and freedom. The door bursts open, and we're through. But then, before we can race off into the dark, Violet is yanked back. I turn, and in the dingy light from the pub, I see Deep Hood's pink tentacle has emerged from the bar and coiled itself around Violet's arm, suckering onto her.

"Herbie!" Violet gasps, struggling as the tentacle begins to pull her back in.

"The coat!" I shout. Vi is still wearing the too-big fisherman's waterproof she took as a disguise. "Shrug off the coat!"

Violet ducks, and the coat slips off her easily, being several sizes too big.

The tentacles pull it away, into the building.

But before we can run, the tentacle flings the coat away and darts out again, seizing Violet's ankle in a vice-like grip.

"It's still got me!"

I grab Violet under the arms and heave, but the thing is strong and my feet slide. I look up and see in the dimness of the corridor a shape darker still – it's Deep Hood, massive and terrifying, filling the doorway. The tentacle is drawing Violet in, and I suddenly know that there's no way I can pull her free. Violet will be lost for sure, and me with her, unless I do the only thing I *can* do.

I let go.

"Herbie!" Violet cries, a look of horror on her face as she is pulled to her doom. But I don't reply.

I'm already running.

Running, that is, back *towards* the doorway. I take the door in both hands and slam it shut with all my force on the tentacle. There's a sickening, rubbery *crunch* – and a roar of pain from Deep Hood. The tentacle releases Violet's ankle, and we burst through the wheelie bins and out onto the cobbles and run pell-mell into the storm-trashed back alleys of Eerie-on-Sea.

We don't stop running till we reach the Grand Nautilus Hotel. Violet dashes for the window to my cellar, which is certainly the quickest way in. But I try to compose myself as I head around to the main doors. We aren't being followed just yet, and I mustn't draw attention to myself. I tuck my uniform in and manage, with some coaxing, to get the sprightning – which is highly agitated – to stop zooming around and hide herself back under my cap. The wind is picking up again, and with the elastic strap broken, I'm going to have to hold my cap in place with my hand. If I'm lucky, I won't bump into Mr Mollusc while I dash back to the Lost-and-Foundery.

"Ah, there you are," says Mr Mollusc as I climb the steps to the great revolving hotel doors. I'm amazed to see him holding the mighty iron hotel key in one hand. "So good of you to finally show up for work, boy. *Just as we're closing.*"

"We're closing?" I ask, ignoring his sarcastic tone.

"But I thought the Grand Nautilus Hotel never closes."

"It doesn't," he says. "But with the storm returning, Lady Kraken has asked me to lock the doors and shutter the windows. It seems we are to become a fortress against the weather."

I look out across the bay. Sure enough, the cloud bank has swollen to fill half the sky, and the angry boom of approaching thunder is already making the cobbles shake. The storm is bearing down once again on the already battered town.

"Does that mean," I ask, spotting a silver lining in all this gloom, "that no one will be able to get in?"

I'm still thinking of the alarming things I overheard the fishermen wanting to do to me, and the idea of the hotel doors being locked overnight is suddenly very appealing.

"Guests will be able to come in," says Mr Mollusc, "by ringing the bell. But all the guests are accounted for in their rooms. Except one."

And he gives a shudder that would tell me exactly which guest, even if I didn't know it already.

"You've picked quite a day for your little holiday, Lemon," Mr Mollusc continues, marching me through the revolving doors.

"Holiday?"

"I have it on good authority that you've been absent from your post all day. Lolling about in Seegol's Diner, I suppose, with that annoying girl. It will be reported to Her Ladyship, of course. And it will be deducted from your pay. Now, get back to work!" And he propels me into the hotel lobby.

Lolling about?

Annoying girl?

Pay?

"Mr Mollusc," I say, drawing myself up to my full height so that I can stare the man straight in the waistcoat button. "I have been out on important Lost-and-Founder business, on The Case of the Fish-Shaped Bottle, which Lady Kraken herself gave me. There has been no lolling."

"You could have fooled me," Mollusc replies, his ridiculous moustache twitching in disgust as he casts his eye over my soggy and battered uniform. "And take your hand off your cap, boy. You look like a little teapot, short and stout."

"But the elastic broke, sir, and—"

"Never mind that." Mr Mollusc locks the revolving doors behind us. Then he turns back to me and waggles the key in my face. "I said, remove your hand."

"But, sir..."

"Do it!" Mr Mollusc snaps, his chins quivering with bad temper. "Now!"

Slowly I lift my hand off my cap and try to hide my panic behind a grin. I can feel my scalp crawling with electrical charge as the sprightning begins to fizz.

Mr Mollusc, still waggling the iron key in front of my nose as he starts to tell me off again, stops speaking. His eyes goggle at my quivering cap.

"What the...?"

There's a flash of *faz-aaap!* and a *ka-ka-BOOM!* of localized thunder as my cap flies straight up into the air. A miniature bolt of lightning leaps into the key, crackling up Mr Mollusc's arm and down into his trousers. His moustache frizzes up like a bottlebrush, and the hair he combs over his head springs straight upright. The manager of the Grand Nautilus Hotel goes stiff as a board and falls over backwards in a puff of smoke.

I catch my cap, jam it back down over the light on my head, and stroll to my cubbyhole, only just remembering to bring the grin with me. Amber Griss, the hotel receptionist, is staring at me open-mouthed.

"Just a little static build-up," I call over to her, pointing at my feet. "New shoes!"

Then I fling up the counter in my cubbyhole and run down into my cellar.

SIDEKICKS AND
SATSUMAS

VIOLET'S ALREADY DOWN THERE, lighting a
fire. Her technique for doing this is to push screwed-
up newspaper and kindling into the iron wood burner,
higgledy-piggledy, and then throw in as many matches
as it takes for the thing to catch alight. I've arrived at the
now-shove-in-a-couple-of-logs-and-hope-for-the-best
stage, so it's too late for me to say anything.

"The hotel doors are locked," I announce. "And my
cubbyhole is closed. I've even pulled down the grille and
locked it. The only way into the cellar now is by the
window, and that's too small for any fisherman to fit
through. My Lost-and-Foundery is the securest place in
all of Eerie-on-Sea. We're safe here."

"I'm sorry, Herbie," Violet says quietly.

"Huh?" I say.

"I shouldn't have pushed you into consulting the mermonkey. I think I still have a bit to learn about the book dispensary."

"Pushed me?" I reply. "Tricked me, more like."

Violet looks sheepish for once, so I let it go. I toss my ruined Lost-and-Founder's cap in the repairs basket and take another from the peg. But I don't put it on just yet. Released, the sprightning flutters around, but, as ever, it always seems to end up sparkling just above my head.

The brass arm and bolt from the clockwork hermit crab is gone from my desk, as expected. Did someone sneak in and take those parts? Or did the hermit crab come and collect them for itself? I prefer the second option, to be honest. That mechanical shell somehow doesn't seem to belong to the horrible world of Deep Hood. I wonder how the tentacled man came by it.

Violet falls back into my big tatty armchair on one side of the fire, and I flop down into the beanbag on the other. I pick up a bowl of odd satsumas – Chef often leaves misshapen fruit out for me – and throw one to Vi. The wind gusts outside as the storm bears down, but in the window of my wood burner, the fire begins to roar, and it's good to be home.

"For a moment back there," Violet says, peeling her satsuma, "when you let go of me, I thought…"

"Ah," I reply. "Then you thought wrong. You're my sidekick, Vi. I'd never leave you in the lurch."

"Wait, I'm not your sidekick." Violet throws a piece of peel at me. "You're *my* sidekick!"

"No, I'm not!" I throw a piece back. "I'm the Sherlock Holmes around here. You're the Watson."

"I'm not the Watson!" Vi shouts, laughing. "Who wants to be the Watson?"

"Well, if you're the Sherlock, sherlock me this: who do you think Deep Hood is?"

Violet pops a piece of fruit in her mouth.

"I thought Deep Hood was hiding his face so he couldn't be recognized," she says after a thoughtful chew, "but after what we've seen…"

I nod. "He's got something more shocking than his identity to hide," I say. "Anyone who can shoot tentacles out of his face is probably not very lovely to look at. I expect he wears that hood just so he can go about in public."

"He must be hideous!" Violet agrees.

"Thing is, though," I continue, after another chew of satsuma, "what are they actually doing wrong, Vi?

Deep Hood and the fishermen, I mean."

"What?" Violet stares at me. "Apart from chasing us this morning? Apart from attacking us on the boat? Apart from saying you should have a 'little accident'?"

I wince.

"OK, *apart* from all that. I just mean that the fishermen sound as if they are planning to stop Gargantis. And if Gargantis, whatever it actually is, is trying to destroy Eerie-on-Sea, are they wrong to want to hunt it? It nearly destroyed the town a thousand years ago. Maybe Deep Hood and the fishermen are right to try to finish the job properly."

Vi shakes her head.

"It's not right, Herbie," she says. "Did Deep Hood sound genuinely concerned about the town to you? No, we're missing something, something important. And besides, since when did drunken sailors making secret plans in smoky rooms over chests of gold ever end well?"

She's right, of course. And anyway, nothing that involves a whaling cannon with explosive spears can possibly be good.

"Whoever Deep Hood is," Violet continues, "he knows a lot about the legend of Saint Dismal. More even than the fishermen, it seems. Maybe even as much as…"

Then she stares at me.

"Old Squint Westerley?" I say, following her train of thought. "Surely you don't think… But Deep Hood *can't* be Squint Westerley, Vi. Blaze saw them both at the same time."

Violet shrugs, but I can tell she knows I'm right. Then she grabs her coat and pulls out the large piece of paper she's been copying Eerie Script onto. She unfolds it across her lap.

"I just wish we could read the secret writing!" she cries in frustration. "I'm sure the answer to all of this is locked in there somewhere."

She stares down at the paper on her knees, as if trying to decipher the code with sheer mental force. Then she ruffles up her hair in frustration and sinks back into the chair.

"It's no good. I just don't get it, Herbie."

I'm about to remind her that even Dr Thalassi can't decipher Eerie Script, despite years of trying, but I'm interrupted by a loud *KLANG-KLANG!* from somewhere up in Reception.

"What's that?" says Violet. "A ship's bell?"

"That," I say, putting my satsuma down, "is the

doorbell of the Grand Nautilus Hotel. Someone's ringing to be let in."

"Who? A guest?"

I get up and pull on the fresh Lost-and-Founder's cap, taking care to scoop the sprightning inside. It's not my job to answer the door, but I feel a little better looking smart and ready anyway. I know who this guest will be.

Deep Hood has returned.

SECRET BUTTONS

AS SILENTLY AS I CAN, I pad up the stairs to my cubbyhole in the lobby and crouch down in the shadow behind the counter. Violet crouches down beside me. Together we peer over – just as we did at the start of this adventure – though this time the lobby is empty. Empty, that is, except for Amber Griss, who is standing behind the enormous wooden reception desk, and Mr Mollusc, who is standing beside her. His moustache is still bushy after his shock earlier. And his eyes are filled with dread.

KLANG-KLANG!

The bell sounds again.

Mr Mollusc sets out across the marble floor with a hesitant tread. But then he stumbles to a halt. The enormous key in his hand starts trembling.

"Miss Griss, p-please see to our guest," he says, turning back to Amber. "Come along, now. Don't keep him waiting."

And he holds out the key with a trembling hand.

Amber throws the hotel manager a narrow look through her severe spectacles, then comes clip-clopping from behind the desk. She takes the key and walks over to the revolving doors. The Mollusc follows, keeping safely behind her.

Amber turns the key and the doors begin to revolve.

Deep Hood stalks into the building, his hood drooping, the metal-bound box swinging, as ever, at his side.

"Forgive us, sir." Mr Mollusc bows excessively. "We only locked the doors against the storm. We are pleased to have you safely back inside our hotel."

And Mr Mollusc leers a desperate grin that says he's not really pleased at all.

"I must see the owner of the hotel," says Deep Hood in his careful, slippery speech. "Immediately."

"L-Lady Kraken?" Mr Mollusc goes so pale he's almost see-through. "But I have already requested that Her Ladyship sees you, and she has declined. She so rarely sees anyone…"

The pink tentacle snakes out from the hood and seizes the terrified hotel manager's tie. He is yanked in close to the gaping hood.

"Tell Lady Kraken this…" Deep Hood says, but his voice trails off to a whisper that we can't hear from our hiding place.

Then he retracts the tentacle with a hiss. I don't even think Amber saw it, it was all so quick. But Mr Mollusc has seen more than enough.

"V-very well!" he cries in a terrified yelp. And he leads Deep Hood to the great bronze elevator, leaving Amber Griss to lock the doors again.

"What was all that about?" says Vi as we creep back downstairs.

"I think," I say, "that what all that was about was me!"

"Do you think she'll see him?" Vi asks. "Lady Kraken seems perfectly capable of saying no to some stranger knocking on her door."

"Yes, but Lady K also loves a good mystery," I reply. "And Deep Hood radiates the stuff. She'll see him in the end."

"Then it's a shame that we can't be there when she does." Violet plants her hands on her hips. "I'd love to be a fly on the wall when that happens. Imagine what we could find out!"

"I can't make you a fly on the wall, Vi," I say, hardly believing what I'm about to say next. "But I might be able to make you a dust mote on the ceiling."

Violet squints at me.

"What's *that* supposed to mean?"

I sigh. I really don't want to do this, but Vi's right – we do need to know more, and this might be our best chance.

"There is a way to see what's going on in Lady Kraken's chambers. But you have to *promise* me you won't make a sound, Vi. Last time we tried eavesdropping you started shouting at the eavesdroppees, and we nearly got tentacled to death."

"Don't remind me!" Violet shudders. "OK, I promise, Herbie. No sound. I'll make no sound at all."

A minute or so later, Violet and I are crossing the lobby towards the hotel elevator. Amber Griss raises one curious eyebrow at me as I appear, but both her eyebrows rocket skyward when she spots Violet coming out of my Lost-and-Foundery just behind. I have to use my cheekiest grin.

"I won't tell if you won't," says Amber with a wink, and she starts shuffling papers as if she hasn't seen a thing.

Amber's definitely on Team Herbie. It's good there's at least one adult around who looks out for me without asking questions all the time.

We step into the elevator, and the polished doors glide shut behind us. Inside, on a gleaming panel covered in decorative dimples, are six numbered buttons:

One for each floor of the hotel.

"Which one do we press?" says Vi. "I've never been in the hotel lift before. Isn't it shiny!"

"It is shiny," I agree. "But these buttons are for the guests. Watch this…"

Arranging the fingers of both hands, I reach over and press all six buttons at the same time. There's an electronic whirring from inside the panel, and one of the decorative dimples spins around to reveal a hidden button. On that button, in tiny letters, it says:

"That's where Lady Kraken lives," I explain. "She has the whole floor to herself, and she does *not* encourage visitors."

"Let's go, then," says Vi, reaching out to press the button. But I catch her arm.

"We can't. Mr Mollusc will be there right now, escorting Deep Hood to her rooms. We need to go here…"

And I rearrange my fingers so that I simultaneously press only buttons one, three and five. Annoyingly, though, my fingers slip, and when the first secret button vanishes and another flips into view, I'm surprised to see:

"Oh," says Vi. "Is that where we're going?"

"Er, no, I made a mistake. I've never seen that one before. Hold on…"

And I press the buttons again, correctly this time. Yet another secret button appears, bearing red capital letters:

"Ooh!" Violet gasps. "Where does *that* go?"

"Press it and see," I say.

"Really?"

And I nod.

So Violet does.

AN ALL-SEEING EYE

"**WHERE ARE WE?**" says Violet as the doors slide open to reveal darkness. I shush her.

"This is the attic of the hotel," I whisper. "It's above Lady Kraken's chambers, and it is strictly off limits. We'll have to tiptoe from here."

"But we can't see anything."

I reach into my pocket and pull out a small key ring torch. It's been in my Lost-and-Foundery for years, so I need to be careful with it. Its owner may yet come back. But for now, its narrow beam of light is just the discreet illumination we need. We step out of the lift, straight onto dusty floorboards.

"There are things here," says Vi, with unease in her voice. "Things in the shadows."

"Watch your step," I reply. "The attic is full of stuff the Kraken family have collected over generations."

I swing the torch around, and its beam picks out carved ceremonial masks, a suit of Japanese armour, a large ornate wardrobe, something like a framed mirror with a cloth over it and a stuffed polar bear with claws and teeth bared. An Egyptian sarcophagus is propped against a life-sized model of a tiger that appears to have some sort of clockwork mechanism. The tiger's eye flashes at us, and I see that the sarcophagus is slightly open. I flick the torch back at the ground and manage not to squeak as I say, "Let's not dawdle."

"This is amazing!" Violet declares, louder than she should. The floorboards creak, despite our best efforts. "I bet Dr Thalassi would give his right eyebrow to get hold of this lot for the museum."

"Probably," I reply, "but I don't think the doc knows what's up here. I doubt even Lady K knows any more. Anyway, what we've come for is over there."

And I flick the torch beam down the long, narrow attic space.

Its light pings off a brass railing up ahead. There's a faint glow of light down there too.

"What is it?"

But I put my finger to my lips, and lead on.

The railing surrounds an opening in the exact middle of the attic floor. It's the top of a spiral staircase. Faint light is spilling up from below, from the corridor that leads to the Jules Verne Suite – Lady Kraken's private residence. And we can hear, from down where Lady K's front door is, the faint whine of Mr Mollusc's voice.

"What's happening?" Vi hisses.

"He's grovelling," I reply, but suddenly I'm less concerned about what's going on down below. My eyes are drawn upwards.

Above us is the tower in the centre of the Grand Nautilus Hotel. Most people in Eerie have no idea what the tower is for – and don't know what Lady Kraken has installed in it – but I do. And it's about time Violet did too. Filling the space in the tower is a strange contraption of gears, levers and oddly shaped lenses. At the apex, surrounded by shuttered windows, is one giant crystal lens, like a great all-seeing eye.

"It's a cameraluna," I whisper, pointing up, answering the question I can tell Violet is about to ask. "Lady K uses it to spy on Eerie-on-Sea. It works by moonlight."

Violet blinks at me in amazement.

I aim the thin beam of the torch upwards at the large

crystal. The light hits it and is deflected out at an angle, criss-crossing between lenses, until it shines back down into our faces. I shut off the torch and rub my eyes.

"Sorry," I say.

"So this is what we've come for?" Vi asks. "This ... cameraluna?"

"Yes," I reply. "I mean, no, not exactly. It's just…"

I look up again. Despite the tower windows being shuttered, the gleam of moonlight is finding its way inside. The wind of the approaching storm is roaring around the roof, whistling through the gaps in the rafters, but for now the sky above the hotel is clear. The moon is still out.

"What's wrong, Herbie?"

Down below, we get a seagull's-eye view of Mr Mollusc's shiny bald patch as he heads back to the elevator, alone.

"Never mind," I whisper. "Come on."

And I lead the way to the far end of the attic.

Here I take particular care not to creak the floorboards, because now we're directly above Lady Kraken's stately sitting room. There's a circular hatchway in the floor of the attic here, kept clear of objects and furniture. Above this is a system of oily gears – designed to open the hatch when the cameraluna is in use – and yet another crystal lens. But that's still not why we're here.

We're here because all around the circular hatchway there is a gap – a finger's width, no more – which gives a surprisingly clear view down into the room below. I found it once, while I was exploring, and I thought it would come in handy one day. It looks as if that day has arrived.

Taking great care to be silent, we lie flat on the dusty boards and peer down into Lady Kraken's private chambers.

As long as Lady Kraken doesn't use her cameraluna while we're up here, we should be fine.

"I am not in the habit of allowing strange men into my rooms," says Lady Kraken, "and if it hadn't been for the claims you make, I wouldn't have admitted you at all, Mr...?"

She's sitting in her bronze-and-wicker wheelchair, at the large round table she keeps directly beneath the circular hatchway in her ceiling. When the cameraluna is in operation, this is where its light projects. And on the table, beside Lady K, is a long-stemmed glass with a little golden wine inside.

"Forgive me, Lady Kraken," says Deep Hood, with a slight incline of his head. He's occupying an armchair on the other side of the table, with the metal-bound box on his lap. His face is still concealed.

"I must maintain my anonymity," he continues. "I assure you, it is for the best reasons. And speaking of reasons, you will no doubt be eager to hear why I have come to you tonight."

"You said something to Mr Mollusc, my manager, about a tincture." Lady Kraken bobs her turtle head suspiciously. "Some sort of 'ocean potion' that you claim can help me. I'll tell you now, Mr Stranger, that I do not buy fandangles from door-to-door salesmen."

"I am no such salesman," comes the gurgling reply, "though I will propose a trade. But first, I believe a little demonstration is in order."

Deep Hood flips the catch on his metal-bound box and lifts the lid.

From our vantage point, Violet and I can easily see the heaps of small gold bars inside, gleaming in the lamplight. We glance at each other. Surely Lady K isn't interested in gold? But then Deep Hood burrows his hand into the treasure and pulls out a tiny bottle, in the shape of a teardrop. He pulls out the stopper.

"My tincture," he coos in his slippery voice as he strokes the bottle. "Unique in the world. Its properties are miraculous."

"That remains to be seen," huffs Lady K, and she picks up her glass in a way that suggests her patience is running out. But what Deep Hood says next makes her look back at him with surprise.

"Tell me, Lady Kraken, how long have you needed a wheelchair?"

"I … I haven't walked for forty years," she replies. "It isn't merely age that puts me in the chair. I have a condition. I do not wish to discuss it. It is incurable—"

"It is not incurable," Deep Hood interrupts. "Allow me…"

The pink tentacle slithers out from his hood and coils itself around the bottle in his hand. In a moment, the bottle is carried across to Lady Kraken, until it is poised over the glass she's holding. With a gesture of surprising precision, the tentacle tips the bottle and delicately shakes a tiny, *tiny* droplet of some fluid from its lip. The droplet lands in the glass, and the tentacle retracts.

The golden liquid in the glass turns purple and strange.

Now, I'll say this for Lady Kraken – she's not easily

flapped. Most people, if tentacled at by a stranger with no face, would be freaking out about now. But Lady K has no flaps to give. It's as if tentacles and potions are all in a day's work for the owner of the Grand Nautilus Hotel. And perhaps they are. The old lady merely raises her glass.

"Bottoms up!" she declares, and gulps down the lot.

She bangs the glass down on the table in a cloud of dust.

"I hope you can see, Mr Stranger, that if your intention in coming here tonight was to try and scare a helpless old lady, then you have failed miserably. I will now ring … to have you escorted … from the premis … prem … ssss…"

Lady Kraken starts to shake.

OCEAN POTION

I ADMIT, I nearly give the game away when I see Lady Kraken convulse. She may rule the Grand Nautilus Hotel like a geriatric dragon up in her top-floor nest – breathing fire at anyone who disturbs her peace – but she's always been good to me. Lady Kraken took me in when I washed up in Eerie-on-Sea. And she gave me my position as Lost-and-Founder, when plenty of others had a better claim to it. There was no talk of "outsiders" from Lady K, just a beady eye sizing me up, and a cap and uniform to wear. So, no, I will not lie here while my benefactor is poisoned!

"Shh, Herbie! No!"

It's Violet saying that, clutching my arm to stop me jumping to my feet.

"Look!" she whisper-shouts, jabbing her finger down towards the gap in the floor.

So I do.

And Lady Kraken is standing. She's standing up!

The embroidered blanket has slipped from her legs, and she has risen to her feet. She teeters a moment, still shaking, but then steps away from her chair.

And doesn't fall!

Lady K embarks on a jerky walk across the sitting room rug, vanishing out of our sight. When she returns to view again, the jerkiness has gone entirely. She's walking normally now, and not only that – she skips her last few steps and then twirls like a ballerina.

"Ta-da!" she cries, looking down and raising each goose-pimply leg in turn to inspect it. The fact that she's wearing nothing but a pair of antique silky bloomers on her lower parts doesn't seem to bother her one bit. "Well, isn't that marvellous? It seems I *shall* go to the ball!"

"I take it you are impressed, Lady Kraken?"

"Indeed!" cries the lady, doing a little jig. "I only wish I really had been invited to a ball. Think of the sensation I'd cause."

"Sadly," Deep Hood continues, "you would still have to be home by the stroke of midnight. This tincture is miraculous, yes, but its effects do not last for long. You will only have use of your legs for a few hours before needing a further dose."

"Then I shall take a dozen bottles," Lady K declares. "Money is no object, and I will buy more when the time comes. You, Mr Stranger, have just found a regular customer."

"*Sadly*," Deep Hood says again, "there is but one bottle. And that bottle, as you have seen, is almost empty."

Lady Kraken stops dancing.

"You mean…?"

Deep Hood inclines his head in confirmation.

"My miraculous tincture, my 'ocean potion', as you call it, is about to vanish from the world for good."

Lady Kraken slumps back down into her wheelchair.

"Unless…" Deep Hood says.

"Unless *what*?" The lady jumps forward again. "You mean, you know where to find more?"

"Not only do I know where, Lady Kraken. I can show you. With the help of your cameraluna."

I look at Violet in alarm.

From down below I can hear Lady K saying, "How

do you know about my cameraluna?" But I can also hear her flipping switches on the arm of her wheelchair, where she keeps the cameraluna control box.

"I know many of the secrets of Eerie-on-Sea," comes Deep Hood's reply, as the gears above us burst into life. "More than any who now lives."

"Get back!" I gasp to Vi, and we slide away just in time. The circle in the floorboards we've been peering around splits into four parts and blooms open like a great wooden flower. Violet has to roll to avoid getting her hair caught in the mechanism.

There's a clanking and creaking sound from the centre of the attic. The shutters over the tower windows are winding open, letting moonlight pour in. A mechanical clicking tells me that the lenses up in the tower are shifting position, gathering up the moonlight and concentrating it into a single beam. That beam fizzes horizontally along the attic towards us, where it hits the large crystal directly above the circular hatchway.

From this last crystal, the light descends into Lady Kraken's sitting room in a cone of rippling illumination, splashing onto the large dusty table below.

Violet is standing now, her disbelieving eyes afire with reflected moonlight. Before I can stop her, she reaches out and touches the ferocious beam that is fizzing and crackling along the length of the attic. She snatches her fingers back and puts them under her armpit.

Cold! she mouths to me.

Now that the gears have settled down, I edge towards the hole again and motion Violet to do the same. If we are careful, we can still watch what's going on below. And when we do look down again, what's going on below is certainly worth watching!

The round table is twinkling with dancing dust motes – tiny points of reflected moonlight that swirl and swarm as Lady Kraken adjusts the controls. Soon three-dimensional shapes begin to form – buildings, streets, the rocks on the beach. A sparkling model of the pier shifts into view, stretching out from a sparkling promenade, with sparkling waves churning around it. It's a living, moving tabletop model of Eerie-on-Sea, made of dust and conjured by enchanted moonlight. I can feel Violet holding her breath beside me.

"So, Mr Stranger," says Lady Kraken, "my cameraluna is at your disposal. What do you wish to see?"

"Do you know of the Vortiss, Lady Kraken?" Deep Hood drools. "I wish to see the Vortiss."

"Of course I know of it!" cries the lady. "My seafaring

ancestors would whirl in their watery graves if I didn't know what the Vortiss was."

And she begins turning levers on her control box.

Below us, the model of the town slips away as our viewpoint moves out to sea. From the attic it almost feels like we are looking down from a hatchway in some airship as it sails out over the ocean. Silver waves pass below us, but soon they are peppered by spikes of rock that rise from the crashing water. These are the infamous Maw Rocks that edge the bay. They grow in size and number as we move further out, forming a complex maze of waterways. But then a gap appears in them. And in the sea that fills that gap, the water turns in a mighty whirlpool.

The Vortiss.

"I hope you aren't going to tell me that this is where your potion comes from," says Lady K. "No one ever sailed near the Vortiss and lived to tell the tale."

"There is one who did," Deep Hood replies. "A fisherman called Squint Westerley. He sailed too close to the Vortiss and was lost ..."

"Of course he was! The fool."

"... but he survived, and he returned with a miraculous tale, and the tusk of a legendary creature."

"Creature?" Lady Kraken asks. "What creature?"

"Gargantis."

"But..." Lady Kraken bobs her head. "But that is the name of a *storm*, not a *creature*. A storm from legend. The locals use the word when the weather gets bad, that's all."

"And yet, there is the tusk," says Deep Hood. "Westerley showed it to me. It is proof, though I lied to him about it. The creature is real."

Violet grabs my arm. We stare at each other. Dr Thalassi said he'd seen this tusk. And Mrs Fossil.

"Bah!" Lady Kraken snaps. "What has any of this nonsense to do with ocean potion and my legs?"

"When I had the tusk in my possession," says Deep Hood, "I was able to retrieve some soft parts. Some flesh. From this I derived a small sample of oil, an oil that has miraculous properties. An oil that you have just sampled, Lady Kraken, and which restored the use of your legs after forty years in a wheelchair."

Lady Kraken has no reply to this. Her head bobs from side to side.

"Still you do not believe me!" Deep Hood splutters with sudden anger. "Show me the storm! With your cameraluna, show it to me!"

Lady Kraken twiddles her controls, and the glittering

dust motes on the table spin and change as the view moves further out into the bay.

Below us on the tabletop, the heaving sea grows dim under a swarm of whirling dust. This dust becomes a boiling cloud bank, which is whipped by a wind that has nothing to do with the atmosphere inside the room. It's the edge of the great storm that is closing in on the town, crackling with lightning.

"My cameraluna cannot pierce the clouds," Lady Kraken says. "There will be little to see..."

She stops.

The wall of cloud parts, and something gargantuan appears.

GARGANTIS!

"A FLIPPER!" CRIES LADY K, pointing a trembling finger. "That is ... a flipper! And fins! And ... and an eye!"

Over the circular table a long, sinuous form coils through the clouds, paddled by a bank of fins along its side. Two enormous flippers, like those of a blue whale but ending in long, curving claws, beat the air, making the storm clouds swirl and spark with lightning. A low-slung mouth, lined with teeth and tusks, gapes below a strange dangling lure that sprouts from the monster's forehead. And in its head vast ichthyosaur eyes roll around, as if searching.

Then the clouds close over this nightmare vision, and it is hidden.

Lady Kraken makes a last desperate turn of her dials, but to no effect. The clouds boil so much that all definition is lost, and soon all there is to see is a swirling billow of dust motes and moonlight over the sitting-room table of an old lady who lives by the sea.

"What was that?" gasps Lady Kraken. "What was that *thing* in the sky?"

"Gargantis," says Deep Hood. "Not the storm itself, but a creature that *causes* it. A storm fish from the lost tales of creation, obscured in the retelling of the Legend of Saint Dismal, but obscured no more. It is the calamity that will destroy Eerie-on-Sea."

There follows a long silence before Lady Kraken speaks again.

"I see now, Mr Stranger, your true intention. You have come to taunt me. You give me back the use of my legs, only to take away all hope. There is no way this storm fish can be caught, so no more of your miraculous oil. And now you tell me my town will be destroyed!"

"There is one in Eerie who has the means to catch Gargantis," Deep Hood replies. "One who has the bait. His name is Herbert Lemon."

"Herbie!" Lady Kraken's turban almost jumps off her head. "My Lost-and-Founder? The dunderbrain?

What has he got to do with all this?"

"The bottle that was brought to your hotel, the one found by the beachcomber and entrusted by you to the Lemon boy? It contained something precious. Something precious to the monster. It is something – maybe the only thing – that can lure Gargantis."

"I have every confidence in my Lost-and-Founder," says Lady K, "to keep that bottle and its contents safe—"

"Lady Kraken," Deep Hood interrupts. "I'm sorry to say that your Lost-and-Founder has given in to temptation. He has betrayed your trust. He has opened the bottle and *stolen* what was inside."

What!

For the second time I almost give the game away. I want to shout, "Hey!" and jump down onto the table and confront Deep Hood. How dare he say I *stole* the sprightning. I didn't steal it – it just zapped out!

And for a second time, Violet grabs my arm.

"Herbie, *shh!*"

I force myself to calm down. Under my cap, the sprightning quivers and sparks as if as shocked and annoyed as I am.

"I ... I don't believe you," declares Lady Kraken. "Herbert Lemon may be a Force Ten ninny about some things, but he has an honest heart. He might just be the greatest Lost-and-Founder we've ever had."

"The matter is easily settled." Deep Hood's voice lowers to an even more sinister tone. "Summon the boy here now, with the bottle. If the bottle remains unopened, I will withdraw my accusation. If, however, there is the slightest opening in the stopper and the bottle is empty, then the accusation stands. In that case, I suggest that you turn the boy over to me so that we may use him to catch the monster."

"We?"

"But of course, Lady Kraken. You will be part of my operation to save Eerie-on-Sea. The monster is searching for this object, and will obliterate the town if it doesn't find it. Every beat of its flippers creates gales; every clash of its tusks begets lightning. But with the object in your possession, we can lure Gargantis to its destruction. The fishermen stand ready to catch it once and for all. And when we are hailed as the saviours of Eerie, and the creature's carcass is beached, I can begin manufacturing my tincture again. You will have a lifelong supply."

One of Lady Kraken's crooked hands reaches towards the button she presses to summon Mr Mollusc. She turns her head to look at it, seemingly surprised to see what it's doing. Her hand trembles above the button as if she's struggling with conflicting emotions.

With a slithering sound, the pink tentacle slides from Deep Hood's hood and creeps towards Lady Kraken's outstretched hand. I just know it's going to press the button for her and summon Mr Mollusc – and my doom.

"There is little time, dear lady," says Deep Hood. "Sometimes you must sail into the storm to find your way clear." And his tentacle, as it approaches her, marks a line of shadow through the silvery dust on the tabletop.

"Clarity Marks!" Violet cries aloud, leaping to her feet. *"Marks* make it clear! That's it, Herbie! That's the secret of Eerie Script!"

"!" I reply, waving my hands in the air as if I can somehow catch these strange shouted words and stop them from reaching anyone else's ears.

But, of course, I can't.

And it's too late now, anyway. I can hear gasps of surprise from the adults below.

"Somebody's up there!" cries Lady Kraken. "In the attic!"

Once again Violet has ruined a perfectly good

eavesdropping session by shouting. Her eyes go wide as she realizes this, too, and she clamps her hand over her mouth.

Down in Lady Kraken's sitting room, I hear Deep Hood jumping to his feet.

So we run. Run, and hope that we can reach the lift before Deep Hood catches us.

I don't bother with the torch – the brilliant beam of the cameraluna is bright enough to see by. We race down the attic towards the elevator, dodging crates and cobwebby furniture.

As we pass the top of the spiral stairs, I hear them rattling. This is the fastest way to the attic from Lady K's rooms, and I imagine Deep Hood dragging himself up these stairs by his tentacle in his fury to reach us. We fly past and sprint for the doors of the elevator.

I jab at the button to summon the lift carriage, but the sliding doors remain closed.

"Someone else must be using it!" I say. "But I've called it and it's coming back up, Vi. I can hear it."

"What about Deep Hood?" Vi says.

I look back down the attic towards the spiral stairs. The sound of feet pounding their way up is louder now, and the railings shake.

The indicator arrow above the elevator doors is almost at the number six.

"Herbie!"

"We can get in the lift, shut the doors and be gone before Deep Hood reaches us, Vi, I promise."

And that's when a shape appears at the top of the spiral stairs.

Silhouetted against the intense moonlight from the cameraluna, it unfolds itself erect on the floorboards – a twisted, crooked figure that steps forward into a moonbeam so that we can see …

… a pair of goose-pimply legs!

"Lady Kraken!" I cry as the owner of the hotel comes into full view.

I'm so unused to her walking that it never occurred to me it would be Lady K who was coming up the stairs.

"Phew!" says the old lady, clutching her back. "Haven't done that in years. Now, then, Herbert Lemon, what are you doing up here? What's all this I've been hearing about you?"

"Your Ladyness!" I say, searching frantically through my grin collection, looking for one to fit this occasion but coming up blank. "But if it was *you* on the stairs, then where is…?"

I trail off.

Right behind us the elevator lets out a cheerful *ping!* and the doors slide open.

"Surprise!" burbles Deep Hood from inside the lift carriage.

Then the tentacle bursts from his hood.

THE BAITED HOOK

THE FIRST THING I NOTICE is how dark it is.

The next thing is that the floor is moving, and everything smells of fish guts and diesel.

Then I find out how much my head hurts, and the rest doesn't matter.

"Bladderwracks!" I gasp. "What … what happened?"

I get a series of flashbacks, between spasms of pain: Deep Hood bursting out of the lift; Violet's terrified face as the tentacle shoves her into the open sarcophagus and slams the lid shut; Lady Kraken's goose-pimply legs as she's knocked head over heels. I remember a flash of icy moonlight in my face as I was bodily lifted up into the cameraluna mechanism. I remember the smashing of glass in the tower as I was pulled out of a window and carried away into the night.

How long ago did all this happen?

When was I knocked out?

And where am I now?

I reach up to my head and feel a lump like a boiled egg nestling in my scrappy locks. My cap is gone.

"H-hello?"

My voice echoes back with a metallic ring.

I hear the heavy throb of an engine and the boom of waves against an iron hull. I know then that I'm on a boat.

There's a crackle of sparks as the sprightning flickers on and takes to the air, right in front of my face, flooding the place with light.

"You're still here, then?" I manage to say, squinting.

There's a crackle of sparks, as if in reply.

"Why have you settled on *my* head?" I demand. "What's so special about me?"

A tiny arc of lightning is my only answer to this. It jumps between the sprightning and one of my uniform buttons, with a *ping* like a little silver bell. Then the little creature plops back down into my hair.

I take in my surroundings. There's a metal door – the kind that has a wheel in the middle to open it. There are piles of plastic crates and fishy nets. I struggle against the rolling motion of the boat, and the rising panic it makes me feel.

"I'm on *Bludgeon*," I say aloud to myself. "Boadicea Bates's ship. I must be."

Despite everything, despite two warnings now from the mermonkey that I will meet a watery end, here I am, once more, on a boat. There seems to be an awful inevitability about the cold, dark bottom of the sea.

I hammer on the door and shout, "Let me out!"

With an ear-splitting creak, the wheel turns and the door swings open. A powerful torch beam shines in my face.

"He's awake," says a voice. "Let's get him ready."

And a rope lasso drops neatly over my head and shoulders. It's pulled tight, trapping my arms, and I'm jerked off my feet and out through the metal door.

"Wouldn't it be easier if he was knocked out again?" says another voice.

"Aye," comes the reply. "The Gargantic Light sticks to him no matter what."

"But it doesn't shine when he's asleep, does it?" says a third voice. "Besides, we might need him to squeak to help attract the monster. He's good at squeaking."

"I can hear you, you know!" I say, but the three fishermen ignore me. We're in a metal corridor now, at the end of which is another door, letting in stormy sea air. All this is lit only by the wondrous light from my head, and the men can't take their eyes off it.

"What do you think will happen to the light?" says the first fisherman to the others. "Once we've used it to catch Gargantis, and saved the day and all."

"I say we keep it," says the second. "Get it back in that bottle and use it to fish with."

"Aye," says the first fisherman again. "Like Saint Dismal himself. We'll catch more fish than ever. We'll be the greatest fishermen this side of Kessel Island!"

"Greatest fishermen *anywhere*," says the third fisherman, "and already heroes for saving the town! I reckon we've got it made."

"I thought you fishermen weren't going out in the storm," I say, trying to get the conversation back to the here and now. "I thought your diesel engines got hit by lightning."

The first fisherman looks down at me reluctantly.

"You thought wrong, then," he says. "Boadicea's put in lightning conductors on *Bludgeon*. Expensive ones. Courtesy of our rich friend with the tentacle."

There's a shout of "Bring the bait!" from the open door, and I'm pulled off my feet again before I can ask anything else. The first fisherman swings me up over his shoulder as if I'm a sack of spuds and carries me out onto the roaring deck. The sprightning dives into my hair again as the wind hits us. Now would be a good time for a blast of lightning, and the electrical sprite *is* crackling in agitation, but it also seems as groggy as I am.

The hardest fishermen of Eerie-on-Sea are gathered there on the deck of Boadicea's great rusty fishing vessel. They gawk at my appearance, but again it's not really me they are staring at.

"The Light! The Gargantic Light!"

I get a view through the spray back along the boat, and I'm shocked at just how far away the lights of shore are. Then, before I can think anything else, I'm swung over and dumped down on the greasy, rain-soaked deck.

"Bring the plank!" bellows a voice I know well. It's Boadicea Bates herself.

A couple of fishermen approach with a long plank that's more than three times the height of the tallest man there. They lay it on the deck.

Boadicea turns to me.

"Lie on the plank!" she commands.

"Don't you mean '*Walk* the plank'?" I say. "I'm not much of a one for boats and that, but even I know that planks are for walking."

"Don't try and be funny," the first fisherman barks in my ear. "Lie on the plank, or I'll brain you with it."

So I lie on the plank, face down, my head over the end. Well, I don't really see what else I can do. Then the sailors lift the plank and the rope lasso is looped around me, lashing me tightly to the wood.

"Still don't seem right," grumbles a voice, as the knots tighten. "Just a kid, that's all."

There's a rumble of uncertainty from some of the other fishermen.

"Since the Light has bound itself to him, we have no choice," Boadicea says, motioning to the fishermen to pick up the plank again, this time with yours truly lashed to one end. "Besides, if he's lucky, he might not get completely eaten."

The fishermen seem content with this.

"Now, run him out the bow!" cries Boadicea Bates.

With this I'm swung forward and shoved far out over the sea beyond the prow of the boat. My head is dangling over the end of the plank, and I'm staring straight down into the churning, inky depths. My ears and hair are blasted back by the wind, and my face is stung by a thousand particles of sea spray as we plough on into the storm. I cry, "Bladderwra-a-acks!" but the word is whipped from my mouth and thrown far away.

I force myself to look up.

The storm is more beautiful and more terrible than ever. Towering mountains of yellow-blue clouds tumble in the skies above, alive with snakes of lightning and metallic clashes of thunder. I see something massive – a shadow – undulate through a gap in the sky mountains, propelled by one vast flipper, before vanishing into the whirling clouds again.

Only a few hours ago I'd have said it was just the spray in my eyes making me see things. But now I know it's not.

I sense the sprightning getting agitated again, crackling as she clings to my hair with tiny fists.

"The bait is set!" The voice of Boadicea reaches me against the wind. "The creature will come!"

"Go!" I shout to the electric sprite above me. "Isn't that what you're looking for? That *thing* up there? Just go!"

But the sprightning clings on.

I look back and see the tall form of Deep Hood emerge from *Bludgeon*'s wheelhouse. He has to hold his hood down against the wind to stop it from blowing back and revealing whatever horrors are hiding beneath.

"The whaling cannon?" he calls. "Is it ready?"

"Aye!" comes a cry, and I see two fishermen braced beside something I never thought I'd see on an Eerie fishing boat: a gun on a swivel mounting – the type once used to hunt whales. Sticking out of it is the lethal point of a spear. And attached to the tip of the spear is something that looks a lot like a grenade.

"Please, just go," I say again to the sprightning on my head. "Please!"

But my voice is lost in the wind as we power through the waves and into the heart of the storm.

THE SIGNAL

IT ISN'T LONG before I'm soaked through. The waves are huge now, and *Bludgeon* is thrown high one moment, only to plunge low the next, racing down the ocean troughs. Sometimes I'm dunked bodily in the sea, to be snapped at by the writhing shoal of fish drawn by the sprightning's light. Then I'm raised high again, as I wobble on my plank, gasping for breath.

My guess is, it's only been half an hour since I was strung up like a carrot on a stick. It feels more like half a lifetime. All I can think is that somehow the mermonkey foresaw all this when it dispensed me *The Cold, Dark Bottom of the Sea* by Sebastian Eels. It warned me, and yet here I am anyway. An image of the cover of that book appears in my mind, but there's an extra little white figure sinking down to be devoured in the depths now. An extra little figure in a Lost-and-Founder's uniform...

Then suddenly the sea stops its crazy rolling. Despite the darkness of night, the sky goes orange and strangely bright, and cloud descends in spiral stacks all around. We are entering the heart of the storm, where even the sea seems cowed into submission. Back on the deck, the crew of *Bludgeon* stare upwards with awestruck faces.

"Make ready the cannon!" Boadicea calls. "Gargantis is close."

I look at the sky, terrified of what I might see.

A shadow-shape coils in the clouds directly above us.

The sprightning, drawing strength from my fear at last, emits a ferocious lightning flash, with her own boom of thunder. Then she fizzes and crackles before emitting a second, even brighter flash.

A zig of lightning zags across the clouds above us with a sky-shattering *KA-BLAM!* that feels a lot like a reply. The sprightning flashes again.

Is she ... *signalling*?

"Look!" calls Deep Hood.

A shadow, darker even than the dark of night, tears the cloud apart. A monstrous fish tail sweeps low across the ocean, sending an angry wind scouring across the surface of the water. The sprightning signals again and again, as something vaster than imagination turns in the heavens.

And that's when I see the eye.

Huge and terrible, a single colossal eye dawns above the cloud bank like a yellow sun rising over an alien planet. A sunspot pupil darts here and there, until it finally fixes on the little sprightning.

And on me.

There's an almighty eruption of triumphant lightning, and the head of the monster is thrown into terrifying relief, its black-hole mouth agape and curling with twisted tusks.

Gargantis!

The monster descends upon us.

"Fire!" screams Boadicea. "For the love of Eerie, FIRE!"

"Wait!" Deep Hood shouts, but it's too late.

There's a *CRUMP!* as the cannon goes off and the spear flies away, directly at the eye. The eye blinks, and the heavens fold as the monster darts away, whirling cloud. The spear vanishes into the maelstrom, and there's a brilliant flash of light – not lightning this time, but the fire of man-made explosives.

A tearing, elemental scream fills the sky as the storm fish takes the hit.

"Too soon!" Deep Hood shouts. "The creature was not close enough!"

"It was close enough for me!" I shout, but I don't think anyone is listening. Everyone is racing around the boat, taking up boathooks and axes, while the whaling cannon is hastily reloaded.

"Bring us about!" cries Boadicea. "It's turning around, getting behind us. Bring us about!"

And sure enough, a long snaky shadow is rippling across the sky from east to west. Gargantis is swimming through the heavens.

I test my hands. I hope that in all the excitement somehow the ropes have been worked loose, but no luck. I'm still tied fast. I feel the sprightning fall back into my hair as if exhausted, her light sputtering.

But Gargantis knows she's here.

There will be no shaking the monster off now. If Boadicea and her men can't kill it, Gargantis will surely devour us, boat and all. I struggle again at the ropes, even more urgently than before.

And I feel something. Something spiky that scratches

my wrist. I look around. Is there a nail or something sticking out of the plank? That's what there would be if this was a story – something sharp I could use to cut through the rope and get myself free. But this isn't a story, and my hopes sink when I see what is actually there.

Standing over my tied hands, on four brass legs braced against the wind, is the clockwork hermit crab. It has one of its sword blades out and is waving it slowly from side to side as it creeps up my back towards my head.

"Aargh!" I cry out, hardly able to believe that my already terrible situation has just got a whole lot worse.

The hermit crab clambers up into my hair.

It lowers itself spikily down my face.

It raises the sword blade till it's just before my eyes.

My mind races. Surely there's a rule of lost-and-foundering for this! But of course there isn't. I screw my eyes shut and get ready to be sliced like salami.

Nothing happens.

I open my eyes and see that the hermit crab is still holding its sword arm out to me. I can see the little gleam of steel, contrasting with the brass, from the bolt I left out on my desk back in my Lost-and-Foundery. I'm going to be cut by the very sword arm I repaired!

But is it taunting me? Or is the hermit crab trying to tell me something?

Suddenly, the shell springs once more into clockwork life. It scuttles back up over my face and head, and down my back to my hands. It begins to saw with its sword blades. But there's no pain. Instead, the constant pressure of the knots vanishes as the ropes are severed and my hands are freed. Then the hermit crab cuts the rope binding my legs.

I'm free!

"He's free!" cries a voice. "The Lost-and-Founder is getting away!"

I struggle to my feet, crouching low on the wobbly end of the plank. I look up at the heavily armed fishermen of Eerie and the reloaded whaling cannon. And I see two things: one thing that fills me with utter dread, and another thing that gives me sudden, unexpected, joyous hope.

The dread thing? Well, that's Gargantis. The monster has swum across the sky way faster than *Bludgeon* can turn, and it is closing in on us from above, like a comet about to collide with the earth.

I look down at the clockwork hermit crab nestling

in my hand. It doesn't have a face, but somehow I know it's looking back at me. Without warning, it jumps in my hand, retracts all its appendages in one smart movement and lands neatly in my jacket pocket.

I rise unsteadily until I'm standing on the plank. I look at Deep Hood, Boadicea Bates and the massed crew of the *Bludgeon*. I look at the descending sky monster.

So this was my destiny after all.

I jump into the sea.

GANCY

I'M UNDER THE WATER for a long time. It's when I surge back up to take a desperate breath that the hand grabs me. Or rather, the *hands* do, as four of them clutch at different parts of my poor, sodden, adventure-soiled uniform and pull me out of the sea.

"Herbie!"

"Violet!" I gasp in reply as I lie on the deck of the *Jornty Spark*.

This, you see, was the other thing I'd noticed – the unexpected, joyous, hopeful thing. The unmistakable shape of Blaze Westerley's little electric boat powering silently towards *Bludgeon* at high speed.

"Welcome aboard," says Blaze. "Now, let's get out of here!" And he jumps back to the wheelhouse. In a second, the *Spark* is banking sharply, sending up a wall of water.

I pull myself up on my elbow and look back at *Bludgeon*. Despite the darkness, I see the fishermen running around in terror as Gargantis falls out of the sky above them. Only Deep Hood stands his ground. He shoves the cowering sailors away from the whaling cannon, swings the weapon up to face the monster and fires. The explosion comes almost immediately in the sky above *Bludgeon*, blasting Violet down beside me. Shattered sea monster scales the size of dustbin lids fall in the sea all around, as the *Spark* roars away at full thrust.

"Vi!" I gasp again, sitting up and flicking a piece of hot twisted metal off my uniform. "How did you find me?"

"We've been out in the *Spark* for an hour, looking for you," Violet replies. "It was the explosions that told us where you were."

"And *Bludgeon*?" I say, twisting around to try and see behind us. "Did the creature…?"

"No," Blaze calls to me from the wheelhouse. "That last spear was a nasty hit. Gancy's been forced back up into the clouds. *Bludgeon*'s still afloat."

Sure enough, Boadicea Bates's boat can still be seen, far behind us as we speed away. There's a beam of light shining out from it, probing the sky. Above her, Gargantis is no more than a coiling shadow, swimming high in the flickering storm cloud. As we watch, a bolt of lightning jabs down at the boat but is channelled harmlessly into the sea. That must be the lightning conductors the fishermen told me about. In reply, another spear is sent skyward, exploding high in the storm, causing a shrieking moan from the beast. *Bludgeon* is waging war against the monster in the sky.

"But why doesn't it just leave? Why's Gargantis still attacking the fishermen?"

Then I remember.

"The sprightning!" I cry. "Where is she, Vi? Did she get away...?"

My mind fills with a sudden image of the fishes that writhed and jumped below me when I was tied to the plank, their awful mouths gaping hungrily at the sprightning's wondrous light. "She wasn't...?"

Violet shakes her head. She holds something out to me. It's a Lost-and-Founder's cap, a dry one that she must have brought out with her from my cellar. I take it and hold it like a bowl. Inside it, the sprightning is huddled in the corner, barely sparking at all.

"She must be exhausted," I say, tipping my cap gently from side to side. "She signalled so hard to go home, Vi."

"Then I hope she perks up fast," says Blaze, powering down the engines and bringing the *Spark* about. "If the sprightning can't signal again soon, Gancy will keep attacking *Bludgeon*. Gancy may be big, but I don't think she'll survive if she keeps being hit with exploding spears like that."

"Gancy?" I say. "You almost make it sound friendly, and not a vast monster out of legend that's trying to destroy Eerie-on-Sea."

"That's because she's not!" Violet declares.

Something's changed. Vi has news, I can tell. And I want to know it! I want to know how Violet escaped Deep Hood and teamed up with Blaze and came out to sea to find me. But I'm suddenly very tired, and the cold of the ocean is shutting down my brain.

I begin to shiver uncontrollably.

"Come below deck, Herbie," says Vi. "I don't care what the doc says, you really might catch your death from this cold."

I must pass out for a bit, because when I can next think straight, I'm a lot dryer. And something is biting my hand.

"Ow!"

"Prr-up!" comes a familiar voice, and a furry head rubs my chin.

"Erwin!"

I'm amazed to see the bookshop cat. On a boat, of all places.

"I needed all the help I could get," says Vi. "When Deep Hood took you, I went into a bit of a panic, and Erwin got scooped up in the rush. But first I had to get out of that sarcophagus."

"What about Lady Kraken?" I say, suddenly remembering her pirouetting underwear as Deep Hood bulldozed straight through her.

"She was all right," Violet explains. "A bit shaken, but that ocean potion stuff was still having its effect. It was Lady Kraken who got me out of the sarcophagus. She gave me a lecture about fandangles and door-to-door salesmen. She'll be fine."

I look around me. I'm still in my battered uniform, and there's an oily towel near by that looks as if it's recently been used to dry off a small Lost-and-Founder. I'm warm and toasty and realize that it's because I'm leaning against the green ceramic battery that powers old Squint Westerley's electric engine. The battery is humming with power, and there's a dependable fizz in the air.

"You fixed it!" I say to Blaze, who is sitting on the steps that lead down from the hatchway.

"Thanks to you two," he says with a grin. "And your advice. Turns out I *could* reverse the polarity of a flow capacitor, after all. If only..." He lowers his eyes. "If only my uncle had been here to see it."

"I'm sure he'd have been proud of you," Violet says, beaming. "And you've piloted the boat like anything, and we found Herbie. You're ready to take over the *Jornty Spark*, Blaze. You've proved it."

But Blaze looks away.

"Why did you shout, Vi?" I demand, bringing her attention back to me. Blaze fixing his uncle's boat is all well and good, but we wouldn't be in this mess at all if Violet hadn't given us away when we were listening in to Deep Hood and Lady K's conversation. "Remind me to never go eavesdropping with you again."

"I know. I'm sorry." Violet pulls a face. "But I suddenly understood something. It was when Deep Hood drew a line across the table with his tentacle that I suddenly understood how the secret writing works. Herbie, I can read it! I can read Eerie Script!"

TWO HALVES OF
A COMPASS

I BLINK AT VIOLET. BUT SHE SEEMS TO BE
expecting something a bit more than blinks.

"Seriously, Herbie," she says. "I can read Eerie Script!
I can read the message on the sides of the fish-shaped
bottle. And the inscriptions on old Squint's charts. I can
read it all!"

"But how?" I say. "What's the secret to reading Eerie
Script?"

Then I think maybe I shouldn't have asked this,
because there's surely no time for an explanation now.
But it's too late – Violet's face breaks out into an excited
smile, and she brings out her piece of paper and pen. I get
the feeling that she's been waiting to tell me all about it
ever since I was kidnapped.

"Herbie, it's easy! Once you know how. Eerie Script isn't ancient runes. It's a secret code, just as I thought. And like any code, you just need to know the key."

"And you've got the key?" I say, though I don't know why I sound so surprised. "You, Violet Parma, have cracked the code?"

Violet nods, sending her hair into overdrive.

"Remember how the symbols never seem to be quite the same from message to message? Well, there are two symbols that are always there. Symbols that look like this."

She smooths the paper on the floor and draws them:

 and

"Yes," I say, "the two crosses, but—"

"What do you get if you put these two symbols together?"

"Er." I overlap the two crosses in my mind's eye and get a funny eight-legged shape. "A spider?"

"No! It's a compass. Look." And Violet draws it.

"It's north, east, south and west from one cross, and from the other, it's the directions in between: north-east, south-east and so on. It's the eight points of a compass, OK?"

"OK."

"Now, remember this?" Violet pulls a book out of her pocket and holds it up to me. It's *Set Course for the Storm* by Clarity Marks.

"That's the book the mermonkey dispensed for me!" I cry, shuddering at the tentacle on its cover.

"Well, maybe it really was meant for both of us after all," says Vi. "Because the title and the author's name are also the clues *I* needed. I just didn't see it straightaway. The key to reading Eerie Script is *direction*, Herbie. So, look at this compass again and tell me which direction you think the storm is."

I look at the drawing.

"North-east?" I suggest. "Because that's the compass direction with the lightning flash?"

"Exactly!"

"Right!" I say, excited now myself. "So what do you do when you have a direction?"

"That's the fun part," says Vi. "You take a pen and make a mark in that direction on every symbol, and then you can read it. It's easy!"

"Um," I say, the excitement going a bit flat. "What?"

Violet shakes her head with impatience. She picks up her pen again and slowly writes a completely new message in Eerie Script, her tongue sticking out in concentration.

"There!" she says, thrusting the paper and pen at me.

"Just draw a short line in a north-easterly direction from every dot."

So I do, feeling slightly silly, until suddenly the Eerie Script transforms in front of my eyes:

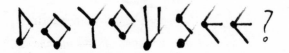

"Bladderwracks!" I cry.

"Bladderwracks indeed," says Vi. "And then, in

another message, you can choose a completely different compass heading, say …

… and leave off parts of the letters in that direction instead, so the code will look different. But as long as you include the compass, anyone who knows the trick will know what to do. That's the secret, Herbie!"

I stare at the paper a bit more, managing to find room in my bamboozled brain to feel amazed by what Violet has done. Then I turn over the paper and look among the scribblings and workings-out until I find the original rubbing Vi made from the fish-shaped bottle. As I thought, Violet has used her pen on this already. I read what it says out loud:

"*Gargantis sleeps, Eerie keeps. Gargantis wakes, Eerie quakes.*"

And then, the message from around the rim:

"*Gargantis dies, Eerie dies, and all falls into the sea.*"

"Gargantis dies, Eerie dies?" I repeat, looking up at Violet. "But that isn't in the old saying. I thought killing Gargantis would *save* the town."

"The fishermen think the same," says Vi. *"Everyone* who believes in Gargantis thinks the same, because this line has been lost and forgotten. But old Squint Westerley found it. Old Squint Westerley understood it all."

"But what about the earthquakes? The cracks in Eerie Rock…?"

"It's not the storm that's causing Eerie Rock to crumble," Vi explains, "it's crumbling because Gancy is out of her cave. *Gargantis sleeps, Eerie keeps*, remember? Squint said the creature was sleeping in a cave when he first saw her. Later he found out why. Gancy isn't destroying Eerie Rock, Herbie. She's been holding it up all these years. If the fishermen kill her, it will be the end of Eerie-on-Sea!"

"But what can we do?"

"The sprightning," says Blaze, "is the Gargantic Light of legend. It's precious beyond anything to Gargantis. We can use it to lure her back home."

"Exactly," says Vi. "We need to lure Gancy away from that whaling cannon, before Deep Hood kills her and causes a disaster."

I look down into the cap in my hands and stroke the little creature gently. At my touch, the sprightning flickers back on and rises unsteadily into the air before plopping fizzily onto my head.

"The sprightning can signal to her," I say. "If she has the strength. But then what?"

Violet gives me a level stare. Then she turns to Blaze.

"Do you have another barrel?" she asks. "And rope?"

"Aye."

"Then I have a plan," Violet declares. "We get the monster to follow us, we sail straight to the Vortiss and lower ourselves down into the whirlpool. Then you, Herbert Lemon, can do your Lost-and-Founder bit and return this Gargantic Light to its rightful owner, once and for all."

THE FIRST RULE

UMBRELLAS.

That's what I thought I'd be dealing with when I took on the position of Lost-and-Founder at the Grand Nautilus Hotel. Umbrellas, and maybe the odd suitcase.

Even when I was first led down into the glittering cavern of misplaced thingummybobbery in the hotel cellar, and had my breath taken away by it all, I still thought the job would mostly be returning whim-whams and knicker-knacks to forgetful guests, and keeping the ledger up to date.

But never, not even in my wildest imaginings, did I think I'd one day face an expedition to the depths of the ocean to return a magical light to a gigantic sea creature of legend.

Of course, I had no one to train me back then. Mr Mollusc just threw my new uniform in my face and marched off, leaving me to cope all by myself. That's why the rules are so important – the rules of lost-and-foundering, which I found scribbled on scraps of paper tucked into the ledger, or pinned to the wall behind the desk in my cubbyhole. One of them even turned up at the bottom of the biscuit jar *(Tea breaks make the world go around. Keep it spinning!)*, another when I was sorting through the lost books on my lost-books bookcase *(One person's throwaway scrap is another person's bookmark!)*. One rule – *Never store snakes in the underwear drawer!* – is even scratched in desperate letters on the floor. It's the collected wisdom of all the Lost-and-Founders before me, stretching back through the ages and coming down to yours truly in countless secret ways. It's the hidden apprenticeship Mr Mollusc will never know I've had.

I've been spending my spare time collecting these rules and trying to get them in some sort of order. I've even tried writing a few of my own. But if there's one thing that unites every rule and makes sense of it all, it's this: *It's not really about the lost things at all. It's about the people who lost them.*

That's the first rule of lost-and-foundering.

If you find something that is lost, and you know who it belongs to, there is NO DOUBT AT ALL what you should do.

Even if it does involve facing your greatest fear and voyaging to the cold, dark bottom of the sea to do it.

I pull my Lost-and-Founder's cap onto my head, sprightning and all, and set it straight.

"OK," I say, with almost no squeak whatsoever. "OK, let's do it!"

We're below deck, helping Blaze tie up the barrel, when something makes us turn. A steady light is spilling down into the hatchway – a light that wasn't there before.

The beam of a powerful searchlight.

"They've found us!" Blaze cries, dropping the rope.

He scrambles up the ladder and onto the deck, with Vi and me running to follow.

Up on deck, the rocking of the boat seems even more pronounced. The waves are growing wild again, and the *Jornty Spark* is being tossed about like a stick in a game of Poohsticks gone horribly wrong.

The deck is floodlit by a powerful beam of light

from across the heaving water. It's from *Bludgeon*, as she crashes through the waves towards us.

"Hold on!" cries Blaze, jumping into the wheelhouse and engaging the battery. The dial lights up a strong blue, and the needle shows a charge of seventy per cent. Blaze shoves the drive lever forward, and Violet and I cling to the rail as the *Spark* thrusts ahead and begins to accelerate.

But *Bludgeon* is already at maximum speed and closing on us fast – an ugly hulk of iron, enveloped in diesel smoke. Its prow slices through the sea like a mighty barnacled blade, threatening to smash our little wooden boat in two.

Blaze spins the wheel, turning us hard to try and dodge the impact. But the *Spark* is struck violently as the great fishing vessel sweeps past and scrapes our side with a sound like splitting planks. Above, on the deck of *Bludgeon*, the fishermen shout and jeer.

"Give us the Light!" bellows the voice of Boadicea Bates over the wind.

Inside my Lost-and-Founder's cap, I feel the sprightning twitch.

But Blaze doesn't reply. Instead he powers down the engine and turns hard again, until we are facing back the way *Bludgeon* came. Then he opens up the throttle to make our escape.

We don't see the rope lasso until it's already over the tusk on the prow of the *Spark* and pulled tight. The other end of the rope must be tied to *Bludgeon*, because we're flipped around as we reach the end of it, and suddenly we're powering straight towards our enemy! Blaze quickly puts the boat into reverse and we start moving backwards, but we're stopped again. It is, quite literally, the end of the line.

"Get that rope cut!" cries Blaze.

Violet and I look around for something to "get that rope cut" with, but there's nothing. Violet grabs the rope and tugs at it, but it's thick and gnarly and strong. In front of us now, *Bludgeon* begins to come about in the heaving water, and the ghastly faces of the fishermen are picked out by flashes from the storm as they leer at us, clutching their axes and boathooks.

The rope begins to shorten as we're winched in.

"The fisherfolk of Eerie," Boadicea Bates calls across the waves, "always make their catch!" And the fishermen roar in triumph.

But now no one on the *Jornty Spark* is looking at *Bludgeon*. It's what's just appeared behind *Bludgeon* that has grabbed our attention. In the sky above, forgotten by the fishermen in their eagerness to capture us, Gargantis attacks. The clouds part, and two vast yellow eyes above a gaping mouth fill the sky as the monster charges down.

"Look out!" we cry to the fishermen, and we point and wave our arms frantically. But the fishermen just laugh and wave back like it's all a joke, as our boat is pulled ever closer to theirs.

Above us, Gargantis – wreathed in storm and lightning – is only seconds away.

"She's going to crush us all!" Violet cries. And it's true – we're so close to *Bludgeon* now that our shared doom is sealed.

Except... I shove my hand in my pocket and pull out the clockwork hermit crab.

"I don't know what part you play in all this," I cry to it. "But if you help me again, I promise I'll do all I ever can to help you!"

The shell springs from my hand, its blades extending in a flash of bright steel. It spins through the air towards the tusk, and with a fourfold sword swipe, it severs the rope.

The *Spark* lurches backwards as we break free.

"Hold on!" cries Blaze, spinning the wheel and then

slamming the drive lever forward to full thrust. Our little boat roars away over the waves at maximum velocity.

I look back and see mighty Gargantis impact the sea where *Bludgeon* is, and where we just were, with a sound like the end of the world. A wall of water – a tidal wave as high as the Grand Nautilus Hotel – soars into the air, and closes over the *Jornty Spark* like a giant mouth in the sea.

DEEP RUNNING

WE ERUPT THROUGH the wall of water, and I am blown off my feet. I find myself hanging on to the boat as pieces of wood and glass from the wheelhouse fly past me. I see Violet, her hair streaming back and her eyes terrified, clinging on by one hand. I grab her and she grabs me.

The giant wave crashes behind us as Blaze squeezes every scrap of speed he can out of old Squint's engine. A surge of water lifts the boat high and carries us with it at a crazy angle. Blaze fights with the wheel, his skipper's cap somehow still on his head as he struggles to keep us straight.

And then, as suddenly as it erupted, the wave is spent and the sea grows calmer, and once again we're just riding the choppy waters of Eerie Bay. Blaze throttles down.

We look around, amazed to be alive.

The *Jornty Spark* is battered, the roof of her wheelhouse torn halfway off. The carved tusk on the prow is leaning at a crazy angle. The turbine has been smashed clean off the wooden pylon, which lies crumpled along the deck. It'll be a long time before the battery can be charged again. But the *Spark* is tough, and we're still afloat.

"*Bludgeon*?" says Blaze, running to the back of the boat and leaning out. "She's … she's gone!"

The sea behind us is empty.

"A direct hit." I adjust my cap. "Deep Hood zero – Gargantis one, by the looks of it. Game over."

"Herbie!" Violet nudges me. "There were people on that boat. And they're … they're all gone. Every one!"

I say nothing. I don't like to think what it must have been like on Boadicea's boat when the monster fell out of the sky and crushed it – and everyone on board – down to the ocean floor.

Then Blaze starts to sing.

It's just a few lines of a song of the sea, sung to a sad tune I've heard before, and it's over almost as soon as it has begun. But he's not singing it for us.

He's saying goodbye.

The fisherfolk may have treated him and his uncle badly, but Blaze is still one of them. There will be few fishermen left in Eerie-on-Sea now.

"We should go," says Vi, putting her hand on his shoulder. "There's something we have to do, remember?"

But I'm not listening. I'm scrabbling around the chaotic deck, shoving aside split boards of wood and twists of metal. *Where is it? Where is it?*

"What are you doing, Herbie?"

"The shell!" I cry. "It's gone. It saved us, and now it's gone!"

"Probably swept over the side," says Blaze.

"But I made it a *promise…*"

"Herbie," Violet says matter-of-factly, "I don't know how you got that shell back, but it's gone now. Just be grateful you had its blades to cut us free."

I sit down on the deck and put my head in my hands.

It's a little later and the storm has given way to strange slow-tumbling clouds in the sky, and the wind has died to a whisper. The ordinary darkness of night reasserts itself, though a weird, wavering glow can be seen below the horizon, as if from the depths of the ocean.

"Gargantis has gone deep," says Blaze. "I reckon she thinks her light was still on the *Bludgeon*. She'll be swimming on the sea floor now, searching, but she'll take to the skies again soon enough, if she can't find it. And the storm will return with her."

He re-engages the engine and nudges the drive lever forward. The *Spark* moves ahead steadily.

"The dial is down to thirty-seven per cent," I hear Violet say. "Will that be enough?"

"It'll get us to the Vortiss at least," Blaze replies, steadying the wheel. "We'll see about the rest later."

Violet glances at me, but I say nothing.

A massive shape sweeps past us on the starboard bow. It's a spur of rock. Shortly afterwards another passes by on the port side, even bigger than the first. We're entering Maw Rocks – the vast expanse of rocky sea stacks that jut from the water like giant teeth. Soon Blaze is having to work hard at the wheel, turning this way and that, as the rocks become bigger and closer together, and the current starts to pick up.

"You know the way?" says Vi.

"Aye," he replies. "I've studied my uncle's charts. And I've been to the Vortiss once before, remember?"

"You think you can find it again?"

"You don't find the Vortiss," says a feline voice. "The Vortiss finds you."

Erwin is peering up at us from the hatchway, his ears flat and his whiskers low. He looks about as uncomfortable on the sea as I am, but amazingly, despite everything, he's completely dry.

"That's true enough," says Blaze, frantically spinning the wheel to avoid a collision with a jagged spike of rock and then turning to look at Vi and me. "But which one of you said that?"

Violet and I point at each other, and I manage a grin.

"All currents in Maw Rocks lead to death or the Vortiss," Blaze continues, turning hard to port. "We've long since passed the point no sailor should pass if he wants to stay alive."

"Why are you speeding up, then?" says Vi. "Shouldn't we slow down?"

"I already have the engine in reverse," says Blaze, twisting the wheel again. "Just hold on. We'll be there soon."

Something big moves beneath the boat.

I look over the side, and my stomach lurches as I see a monstrous, glittering flank of scales and fins slide along deep, *deep* beneath the water, leaving me with an impression of vastness and deepness that makes me want to close my eyes and not open them again till we're back on dry land.

"Gargantis!" says Blaze with a gulp. "Still searching. She would break us like matchwood if she surfaced now."

I clutch my Lost-and-Founder's cap. I can feel the sprightning twitching inside, prickling my scalp with her electrical potential. Has she rested enough to signal? And am I really about to be lowered underwater in a barrel to return her to this giant of the deep? Oh, bladderwracks! I am, aren't I? I think my knees are about to give way.

Then we pass between two great horns of rock and see before us an amazing sight.

VORTISS

A SPACE OPENS AHEAD – a clearing in the treacherous expanse of rocks. But the sea here is far from calm. Fed by converging currents, the water is channelled around and around, spiralling into a rushing whirlpool wider than the Eerie pier is long. And at the centre of the whirlpool, the water turns and falls away into a gaping black hole.

The Vortiss.

Almost as strange and terrible as what we can see is *how* we can see it – myriad points of light are zipping around in the air, or drifting on the wind, or dancing across the water's surface, bathing everything in a magical, sparkling light.

"Sprightnings!" Violet gasps. "Dozens of sprightnings!"

Blaze pulls the drive stick back to full reverse, and we come to a stop – holding our position against the current between the two great rocks. All that is keeping us from being sucked into the powerful whirl of the Vortiss is old Squint's engine and the mighty battery he built to run it. I glance at the dial. Its needle is trembling on twenty per cent.

"These ones seem different, though," says Vi, as the sprightnings gather around us, zipping here and there. "Smaller, more like electrical bees."

"They don't look too friendly," I say as one of the crackling things zaps off the rail beside my head with a *pang*, showering me with sparks.

"Ow!" cries Violet, ducking as another swoops low and singes her hair.

"Gancy's been hurt," says Blaze, dodging an electrical sprite of his own. "Maybe they think it's us who did it!"

Then three sprightnings fly down through the open hatchway and go *ping-pang!* as they zip around the pots and pans below deck.

"They're trying to get into the engine!" cries Blaze.

But before he can act, they fly back out and circle the boat once before spiralling in towards my head.

I feel a tugging at the elastic on my Lost-and-Founder's cap.

So I take it off.

The sprightning – *my* sprightning – leaps from her hairy hideout and dances joyously above my head. She lets out a flash of lightning. The other sprightnings flutter close, sparking bright and dancing in the air. They start flashing, too, as if amplifying the signal.

"Oh!" Violet shouts, pointing into the sky above us.

I lift my head and nearly fall over.

Above the *Jornty Spark*, filling the sky over the Vortiss, the vast face of Gargantis looms down at us – two immense half-moon eyes over a huge tusk-edged fishy snout. Behind it, a long sinewy body coils and turns gently in the air, as hundreds of shimmering fins flutter and bat, creating clouds. On either side of its neck, gigantic flippers paddle slowly as the beast comes to a halt just above our little boat and treads the air.

"Gancy!" Violet climbs the broken wheelhouse and reaches out, managing to touch with one fingertip the gnarly, chinless lower lip of the mighty storm fish. The creature lets out a long, keening moan in sing-song response.

On Gancy's head, between her eyes, is the stem of

a lure, like the lure that protrudes from the head of an anglerfish. At the end of this stem is a large gauzy bulb, like a sling, open on one side. But unlike an anglerfish, whose lure glows bright, Gancy's is cold and dark.

My sprightning – the Gargantic Light – starts dancing above me, and I suddenly realize exactly what I need to do to return her to her rightful place. And I could shout for joy, because now I won't need to be lowered down into the ocean's depths in some smelly old barrel! I can return the light right here, right now, and get the lost-and-foundering done when I'm only *half* drowned! And then, when the day has been saved and the world put to rights, we can sail back to Eerie-on-Sea to see if Mrs Fossil still has some of those salty caramel muffins left!

I climb onto the ruins of the wheelhouse beside Violet. The creature must sense what I'm about to do and lowers the bulb of its lure towards me. I cup the sprightning in my hand and reach up as the empty bulb swings down.

But my hand doesn't get there.

Gargantis lurches back as a spluttering, roaring sound cuts through the night – an angry mechanical noise that seems offensive in this mythical moment.

A hulking shape emerges into the sea clearing, in a cloud of stinking diesel smoke.

"It can't be!" gasps Blaze.

But it is.

It's *Bludgeon*.

The iron fishing vessel is crumpled and buckled, and its masts and spotlights are smashed. Smoke spews from twisted gaps in the hull, and the boat is barely afloat at all. And yet, somehow, *Bludgeon* has survived! On her deck the wild faces of the fishermen stare in terror at the creature above them.

All except one.

Deep Hood points the whaling cannon towards Gancy and fires at point-blank range.

The spear hits the creature in the neck, embedding itself deep. Then the bomb on the point explodes in a sickening ball of fire that bursts out of the storm fish's mouth.

"Gancy!" Violet cries as the great beast writhes and twists, shrieking with pain and spouting flame. It smashes a flipper into the sea, and I fall back off the wheelhouse and crash to the deck. The sprightning spirals helplessly back down towards me, as if tugged by an invisible string.

"NO!"

Gargantis tries to rear back into the clouds, shattered scales tumbling from her wound, but instead she starts falling from the sky, her fins going limp, one by one. There's a crash of splintering rock as she smashes into a sea stack and collapses into the sea.

"What have you done?" Violet wails towards *Bludgeon*.

It's then that the other, smaller sprightnings attack. They swarm around the iron fishing boat, darting and zapping at the fishermen and running in hot angry arcs across its surface. Deep Hood is struck full force and drops from sight with a cry, his tentacle flailing. Then they reach *Bludgeon*'s diesel engines, and there is an explosion as the back of the boat is blown wide open.

The fishermen cry out in terror as their vessel, no longer under power, is instantly grabbed by the fierce currents of the Vortiss. *Bludgeon* sweeps around the whirlpool once, then twice, and then – on the third turn – is pulled decisively into the centre. The boat tilts crazily and then it's gone, all thousand tonnes of it, swallowed with its crew by the relentless swirl of the Vortiss.

"They've killed her!" Violet clutches at me. "They've killed Gancy!"

The CHARGE dial starts flashing a warning, the needle dangerously low.

"We have to go!" Blaze cries, grabbing the drive lever. "Or the Vortiss will get us too!"

Then something breaks the surface of the swirling sea and towers above us, streaming water. It's one of Gargantis's mighty clawed flippers. Before we can react, it sweeps down and strikes the side of the *Jornty Spark* with a tremendous smack.

And now I'm flying through the air.

Except, of course, that Lost-and-Founders can't fly, not on their own, so the actual flying part is soon over, and I hit the sea before I can close my mouth.

When I bob up to the surface, flapping my arms and spluttering for breath, the *Spark* is far away, turning wildly, and I'm already deep in the irresistible current.

"Blurbie!" glugs a voice, and I see Violet close by in the water, reaching out to me. I reach back and we cling together as the world turns and turns and turns again, as we're swirled into the mouth of the Vortiss and swallowed down to the cold, dark bottom of the sea.

THE TURGID LAKE

"HERBIE! HERBIE, WAKE UP!"

Wake up? How can I "wake up"? I don't remember going to sleep. I do remember something, though. Now, what was it? Ah, yes…

OH!

I wake up with a start.

"Herbie, you won't believe where we are." Violet's wet hair is all over my face as she blinks down at me. "Look!"

And so I do, propping myself up on one elbow and staring around.

"The bottom of the sea!" I gasp.

Beside my elbow is a human skull.

"Argh!"

"Herbie, calm down!" Violet snaps. "Look a bit more."

I force my eyes off the skull and gaze around.

I'm lying on a bed of soft mossy earth, in an other-worldly landscape that is dotted with strange plants and lit by the glow of sprightnings. All around are the wrecks of ships and boats, more than I can count, some ancient beyond belief. The ground is littered with coils of rope, anchors, cargo barrels and other ship's whatnots – looking like they have been flung here over centuries.

"It's not the seabed, Herbie," says Vi. "It's a cavern! A huge undersea cavern, beneath Eerie Rock."

I get to my feet, gaze around the vast space and see that the wrecks are lying on the shore of a lake of churning water. Arching over it all is a high rocky ceiling, sparkling with stalactites and echoing with the sound of the splashing lake. Sprightnings flit and crackle here and there, and at the far end – in the cavern wall – I see the openings of caves.

"I think that's the other end of the Vortiss," says Vi, pointing to the seething lake. "Where the things it swallows are spat out."

"Like we were?" I ask.

"Aye," says a voice I don't recognize. "Like a pair of shrimps sucked into the belly of a whale."

We spin around to see a wiry old man dressed in tatty woollens and an old weather-beaten waxed coat. He has a wild beard, even wilder hair and some pretty wild tattoos. The little spectacles on his nose are much repaired.

"Are you …?" Violet begins.

"… old Squint?" I finish. "Old Squint Westerley?"

"Aye," says the man. "But less of the 'old', if you don't mind. I'm as fit as a gazbaleen's girdle, I am!" And he thumps his chest, causing a small coughing fit.

"Now, what's all the noise?" he asks, when the coughing has subsided. "And how did you…?"

Then he stares behind us, his eyes nearly popping out of his head.

"By Dismal's beard, Gancy! Gancy's back!"

And now he's running between the wrecks – if you can call jogging from one crooked leg to the other running – and so, of course, we run after him.

Gargantis, when we reach her, is lying in vast and spectacular ruin, at the edge of the lake. Her great length is coiled and collapsed in the water, deflated like a crashed airship, her banks of fins lying limp. Her jaws – bristling with tusks – are closed, and her wounds are terrible to see.

One barnacle-encrusted eyelid is open a little,

showing a wide yellow slit through which she gazes down at us as we gather beside her. She lets out a long, keening moan of pain.

"She's still alive…" says Violet.

"Barely!" cries Squint. "Oh, disaster! Who did this?"

Violet and I look at each other. Where do we even start explaining everything that's happened? But then Squint looks past us, and his eyes darken as they narrow.

"Ah, of course," he says. "I might have known."

Behind us, on the far bank of the lake, the wreck of *Bludgeon* is resting at a crazy angle, its whaling cannon smashed. All around, the fishermen of Eerie are sitting dazed or staggering in the shallows. As they regain their senses, they stare in wonder at their strange surroundings and the stricken monster they helped to destroy.

"This is all my fault!" Old Squint tugs his beard. "I should never have told anyone about this place till I understood it all myself. I should never have told anyone about Gancy. And now nothing can keep Eerie Rock from sliding into the sea."

"There must be something we can do!" cries Violet.

Squint Westerley shakes his head.

"Without the Gargantic Light, there's nothing any-one can do."

"The Light!" I shout. "The sprightning! I had her with me, but..."

"*You* had it?" The old man grabs me by the scruff. "Is it here? Where is it now? Quickly, boy!"

"I ... I don't know." I pat myself down and clutch at my capless head. "It was following me around, but ... but..."

"Herbie, keep still," says Vi. She reaches towards my ear with a little driftwood stick and then gently hooks something out from behind it and drops it in my hands.

In my palm the tiny, sodden figure of the sprightning lies motionless, not even the slightest spark of life crackling from it.

"By Dismal's beard!" gasps old Squint. "Quickly, she must be returned to her nest! It may be hard to believe, but the fate of great Gargantis and this tiny sprightning are deeply entwined. If we can get them back together, there may still be time."

"Nest?" says Violet. "What nest?"

But Squint is already at the front of Gargantis's head, beckoning me to join him. The long, spindly appendage of Gancy's lure lies drooping down the front of her head, the empty bulb at the end limp on the ground.

"The sprightning gives light to the storm fish, and Gargantis gives the sprightning electrical power in return, so she can breed her swarm. They bind for ever, and should never be separated for long. While one lives, there's still a chance for them both. Quickly!"

I walk over to him, cupping the little creature in my hands, blowing on her gently, willing the fairy back to life. And she crackles in response – the tiniest spark of a wing – and begins to glow faintly again. Behind me, the fishermen of Eerie gather around.

"Who *are* you?" says old Squint in a wondering voice, as he watches the light brightening in my hands.

"Me?" I say. "I'm Herbie, Lost-and-Founder at the Grand Nautilus Hotel. This light – the Gargantic Light – was lost. I'm just trying to return it to its rightful owner, that's all."

And I crouch down beside the bulb on the ground.

"This belongs to you, Gancy."

I nestle the faintly glowing sprightning inside the gauzy bulb and take my hands away.

The light of the sprightning flickers out and dies.

There's a hush over the fishermen, and over me and Vi, too, because it seems as if something should be happening now, only something isn't.

Then the ground starts to shake.

HORRIBLY CHANGED

THE SHAKING OF THE GROUND intensifies, and all around us stalactites begin to fall from the cavern roof. Straight in front of Gargantis, as if the creature had been trying to reach it, there is a large cave entrance in the cavern wall. The rock around this cave cracks and splits, as if the whole cavern wall was collapsing under its own weight.

"We're too late!" Old Squint's face goes deathly white. "Eerie Rock is crumbling. Gancy's been out of her cave too long. The whole thing is going to come crashing down!"

"But Eerie-on-Sea is built on that rock!" I cry.

"What about them?" Vi says to Squint, pointing to the other sprightnings. They are flying around the cavern in great agitation. "Won't one of those do?"

Squint shakes his head.

"It has to be the queen, the one that fool Dismal trapped in the bottle. Those others are just her children, the workers of the swarm, who guard the Vortiss."

"Come on!" I crouch down and pat the gauzy bulb, feeling useless. I can see the tiny fairy figure lying in there, motionless, without a spark. "Come back! I returned you to your home. What else can I do?"

Then Violet starts to sing.

Now, I'd like to say that Violet has a beautiful voice. I'd like to say she sings like a Disney princess, and that wild creatures gather around to listen, but that wouldn't be true. It's not a *bad* voice – don't get me wrong – it's just a creaky, uncertain one. Like the voice of a person who never normally thinks to sing, and who is astonished to find herself doing it now.

I look up at her and see a tear in her eye. She has one hand on Gancy's side.

Violet's song is the one I've heard the fishermen sing as they fix their nets and set their sails, and it's the one the clockwork hermit crab played for us back in my cellar, at the beginning of it all. It's the same song Blaze sang when he thought *Bludgeon* was lost – an old, sad song of the wind and the waves and the sea.

But Violet doesn't know all the words.

The song dies mid-verse, and now Violet's mouth is just opening and closing as she desperately tries to remember more.

So the fishermen sing it for her.

One by one, the burly, sullen fisherfolk of Eerie-on-Sea take up the song where Violet leaves off, their voices raised in harmonious chorus. Even Boadicea Bates joins in, her voice surprisingly high and clear. The fishermen reach out and touch Gargantis, and close their eyes, and sing.

Until the song is ended.

And Gancy lies as still as stone, her light extinguished.

"You're too late!"

A horrible voice cuts into the silence, enunciating each word with disgusting precision. Deep Hood steps out from behind the wreck of *Bludgeon*.

"The creature is dead! And now I will have its carcass."

"You!" cries old Squint. "Oh, what a fool I was to trust you with the secret. Now look what you've done!"

"You never would have discovered any secrets without my help," Deep Hood sneers in reply. "Without my gold, you'd still be tinkering on your boat with that dim-witted apprentice of yours."

Squint Westerley unhooks an axe from his belt and hefts it threateningly.

"Blaze is no dimwit! He's just not ready, that's all. One day he will be, and then I'll teach him about all of this."

The ground starts shaking again, and boulders fall down the rock face.

"But there won't be a 'one day', will there?" Deep Hood gurgles with laughter. "Eerie-on-Sea is doomed."

"Why?" Violet shouts. "Why have you done this? Just to make your stupid potion?"

"Stupid?" Deep Hood roars in fury. "Who are you to call me stupid, Violet Parma? It's thanks to *your* stupidity that I'm here at all – that I have to do any of this."

"What do you mean?" I say, joining Violet at her side. "Who *are* you?"

"Do you really not know?" Deep Hood swings his hood from me to Violet and back to me again. "Have you already forgotten? Forgotten how you stopped me from getting my prize once before? How you left me to die in the bowels of a battleship, torn to shreds by the malamander, my hand bitten clean off?"

Violet gasps.

"But the oil of a storm fish is miraculous. It grew back that hand!"

He lifts his right arm, and the sleeve falls back, revealing a hand – shiny pink, as if newly grown.

"And a few little *extras* besides."

The tentacle slides out and waves obscenely in the air. Then it throws back the hood, revealing a face we thought we'd never see again.

The author of *The Cold, Dark Bottom of the Sea*.

Sebastian Eels.

Standing before us.

But the once-handsome face of Eerie-on-Sea's most famous writer is horribly changed: around his mouth, dozens of little pink feelers wave in the air and clutch at his lips and gums. No wonder he sounds as if he's struggling to speak. On his neck, gills gape and twitch, as if desperate for water, while behind his head the repulsive pink tentacle rises triumphantly from between his shoulders.

"Oh, I was shocked too," he says, seeing our faces. "When it first happened. But then I realized just how useful extra limbs could be."

Violet, the fishermen of Eerie and I – we all recoil in horror.

"And this is just the start!" drawls Sebastian Eels. "With more of my tincture, what could I become? Stronger, even, than this? Faster, tougher – something truly magnificent?"

"You have sold your humanity," says old Squint in disgust, "to become a monster."

Sebastian Eels spits a gob of green saliva.

"Humanity is cheap," he burbles, "and so easily *crushed*."

Without warning, the tentacle strikes forward and punches Squint in the face. The old fisherman is knocked to the ground, his glasses shattering.

Eels picks up the fallen axe with his tentacle and twirls it expertly as he faces me and Violet.

"And now it's your turn."

DEEPEST SECRET

AND SO WE RUN – me to the left, Violet to the right. The axe zips between us and bounces off the hard scales on Gancy's snout.

I don't know how, but without agreeing in advance, Violet and I are both running to the cave entrance we saw in the wall of the cavern. Eerie Rock may be about to collapse – the ground is shaking harder than ever – but the cave seems to offer more places to hide than anywhere else. We reach the mouth of it, gasping for breath, looking frantically behind us for signs of pursuit.

"Where's he gone?" I gasp.

"I don't know," cries Vi. "I can't see him!"

Drip.

A drop of green lands on the rocks between us.

Drip.

Another blob of green. This time on my shoe.

Slowly, Violet and I both look up.

Above the cave entrance, staring down at us with dark glee, Sebastian Eels is suckered onto the rock by his tentacle, his hands and feet planted against it, ready to strike. Another glob of green saliva falls from his terrible grin.

We back into the cave, stumbling and tripping, as the man-become-monster drops powerfully onto the rocky floor and turns to face us.

"Am I not beautiful?" he gurgles. "With more of my tincture, can you even *imagine* what I might become?"

"But the town!" says Violet, as we back further into the cave. "Without Gancy to hold it up, Eerie-on-Sea will be destroyed! Don't you care?"

"A ridiculous place full of meddlers and simpletons," Eels says, stalking into the cave entrance after us, tentacle poised like a scorpion's tail. "Of course I don't care! It will be easier for me when everyone is dead, and nothing but skeletons at the bottom of the sea." He flashes a knowing glint at me as he says this. "Easier for me to locate the deepest secret of Eerie and take it for my own."

"Deepest secret?" I say. "What 'deepest secret'?"

"You know, it's actually funny," says Eels as he drives us further down the cave. The whole place trembles again, and rocks fall all around, but Sebastian Eels just deflects them with his tentacle. "Funny that you, of all people, Herbert Lemon, don't know the secret. Everything truly eerie in this place is tied together by a common thread – the malamander, Gargantis, a cat who can speak…"

"What?" cried Violet. "How do you know about Erwin…?"

"Oh, I know. I know more about the legends of Eerie-on-Sea than anyone. And that includes the story of the boy who washed up in a crate of lemons."

"*You* know my story?" I can hardly believe what Eels is saying. "You know where I come from? But … *how*?"

"I could tell you." Eels gives a superior smile. "But you're about to be dead anyway, so what does it matter now? Ha! Just think, you survived the sinking of SS *Fabulous*, only to end up axed to bits in this dismal cave."

My mouth falls wide open.

"SS *Fabulous*?" I cry.

I'm about to add, *But that's the name of the ship in your book!* but suddenly there isn't time. There isn't time for anything.

Because, back down by the lake, I've just seen something that makes me jangle from noggin to niblets with both terror and hope.

Behind Sebastian Eels, out in the cavernous undersea landscape, something massive is rushing at us on frantic flippers and fins, closing fast, a powerful light blazing between two huge yellow eyes. Something that is about to enter the cave like a speeding train enters a tunnel.

Gargantis!

Revived!

I see a deep, wide fissure in the cave wall beside us. With barely time to think, I shove Violet into it. Well, there's no need for us both to be squished, is there?

Eels' face changes as he realizes what is about to happen.

But it's too late.

Gargantis enters the cave in a blaze of light and a roar of scraping scales and fins, her gaping mouth scooping up Sebastian Eels, boulders of rock ...

... and me!

Somehow I manage to grab a tusk and cling on, my legs dangling down inside the throat of the storm fish as she powers deep, deep into the caves beneath Eerie Rock. Further down that throat, eyes wide with terror,

Sebastian Eels clings by the tiniest tip of his tentacle to one of Gancy's massive teeth.

"Save me!" he screams, his voice just reaching me above the crash and roar. "Save me, Herbert Lemon, and I'll tell you who you really are!"

I blink as stones bounce down my face and arms. I try to get my foot towards him...

Then the tentacle gives way, and Sebastian Eels flies down, down into the eternal dark of the belly of Gargantis.

There's a sudden echoing sound and change of air, and the creature's head bursts out through a second cave entrance. She comes to an abrupt halt, and I'm thrown forward and out of the monster's mouth, to land upside down and back to front on a tuft of prickly sea lavender.

"OW!"

GUARDIAN OF GARGANTIS

I PICK MYSELF UP and pull out a spiky twig or three.

"Herbie!"

That's Violet calling.

"Herbie, are you OK?"

She's running across the mossy ground. Behind her is old Squint Westerley, clutching his bashed face. It's then I notice that the cave Gancy's head emerged from is only a short way from the one we first entered. Despite this, Gancy's entire body is now concealed, threaded through the foundations of Eerie Rock.

The storm fish sings a deep, melodious note and snaps her jaws once or twice. There's a rushing sound as air is drawn into her mouth, and I sense her long body inflating and filling the cave beneath Eerie Rock completely. The trembling of the ground stops, and the rock face falls still. Then Gargantis twists her tail over towards her head, gently closes her mouth over it and allows her eyes to close. As we gather around, the breathing of the great storm fish settles into a slow, peaceful rhythm.

Above Gancy's head, at the end of the lure that sprouts between her eyes, the gauzy bulb bathes us in a twinkling glow.

"She sleeps!" says old Squint. "At last, Gargantis sleeps."

"So Eerie keeps?" I ask, and the old man smiles.

"There's someone who doesn't sleep, though," says Violet, pointing. The sprightning crawls out from the opening in the side of the bulb. Her electrical wings spark on, and she takes to the air, flitting around with a bright crackle of energy. All the other sprightnings in the cavern swarm around, darting here and there, but ours – the queen of them all – shines the brightest and the fiercest.

"She looks better than she ever did nesting on my head," I say.

Then she notices me and flitters down to bob in front of my face.

I reach my hand up, but Squint blocks it.

"Don't touch her," he says. "She's bound herself to her storm fish again, where she belongs. It's people touching her and putting her in bottles that started all this trouble in the first place."

The sprightning – *my* sprightning – hovers closer still, and somewhere deep inside her brilliant light, I think I can see a little fairy face smiling out at me. And then she's gone, whirring away back into her nest on the head of Gargantis. The gauzy bulb glows again with a wondrous light as the other sprightnings dance around.

"But what about Gancy?" says Violet. "Is she going to be OK?"

Old Squint gives a pirate's grin and pats the storm fish's snout.

"She's an ancient thing," he replies. "A creature from the beginning of the world, who should endure till its end. I reckon she'll heal well enough. But she'll need looking after."

"Like Saint Dismal looked after her?" says Boadicea Bates, approaching with the other fishermen. "In the old stories?"

Squint grunts.

"No. Not like that at all."

"What happened exactly?" Violet asks. "When you

brought Deep Hood here? Blaze told us his side of it, but…"

"Blaze? You've seen my nephew?"

"It was Blaze who brought us here," I reply. "In the *Jornty Spark*."

Squint looks amazed to hear this. Then he shakes his head.

"I was such a fool. I was desperate to finish my engine, but I should have realized that the man in the hood meant no good. Yet I took his gold and agreed to take him to the Vortiss. I suppose I was just pleased to meet someone who didn't laugh at my stories." And he glares at Boadicea. "Anyway, I realized my mistake soon enough."

"Because of the bomb?"

Squint nods.

"I couldn't believe it when he pulled it out. I fought him, but that tentacle burst from his hood and threw the bomb at my boat! I understood then that he wanted to kill us so that no one else would know he was here, or how to find the Vortiss. I had no choice but to cut the rope that held the barrel and hope that Blaze would have the sense to get away."

"He did," says Violet.

"Anyway, when we got down here, the fight continued. That hooded maniac threw another bomb, right at Gancy's head! He seemed desperate to kill her before she could wake. That must have been when the fish-shaped bottle got thrown into the water and lost. Well, there was no stopping Gargantis from waking after that. Sebastian Eels fled for his life back out to sea, leaving me here, desperately trying to find that bottle. It must have been washed into the sea as well."

"It turned up on Eerie Beach during the storm," I explain. "I've been trying to figure out who it belongs to ever since."

"And we never would have done that without Blaze," says Violet. "He was amazing."

"Was he?" Squint looks taken aback.

Violet gives the old man a stern look. "He fixed your damaged engine all on his own, and he stood up to the other fishermen. *And* he sailed the *Jornty Spark* into Maw Rocks to bring us safely to the Vortiss."

"He even reversed the polarity," I say, "of a ... a ... thingummybob. And everything!"

Squint Westerley opens and closes his mouth as if stunned. Then he looks up at the stalactite roof of the cavern to the deep sea beyond, and nods.

"That's my boy," he says.

"How did the sprightning end up in a bottle in the first place?" I ask then. "It seems so cruel to lock her up."

Squint scowls.

"As for that, we have no one to blame but old Dismal himself. Follow me."

So we do, as he climbs rough-hewn steps in the cliff. We arrive at a recess – a shelf of rock just over the cave entrance where Gancy's head now trembles with profound snores. In the recess, sitting on a throne made of boat wreckage and storm fish tusks, sits a skeleton – a skeleton wearing the crumbling remains of a monk's habit. On the chin of the skull, attached to scraps of mummified skin, is a long dangling beard that reaches all the way to his bony toes. By the way the skeleton's arms stick out, you can tell that something used to be held there.

The fish-shaped bottle.

"Is that...?" I goggle at the remains. "Is that Saint Dismal?"

"Aye," says old Squint, straightening the saint's wonky skull and brushing rock dust from the top of it. "But *Saint*? My armpit! He was nothing but a thief who found this place by chance and stole the Light. But when the Light is taken too far from a storm fish, the storm fish will wake. Gargantis searched in storm and rage to get her sprightning back, and Dismal realized he had no choice but to return it. The town was being destroyed. If only he'd left it at that, none of the rest of it would have happened."

"What do you mean?"

"I mean, he took the Light again. And again and again. He couldn't resist it. Dismal was a fisherman, and there's nothing quite like the light of a sprightning for attracting fish. That's how a storm fish fishes, after all, during its prodigious once-a-century hunts. Put a sprightning in a bottle and dangle it in the sea, and your nets will fill to bursting. Dismal found that as long as he brought the sprightning back to the cavern before dawn, Gargantis wouldn't fully wake. It was a risk, but Dismal became famous for his miraculous catches. People came from far and wide to venerate the First Fisherman of Eerie-on-Sea and his wondrous Gargantic Light.

"But in the end he got fearful that someone else would take it. He couldn't stand that someone in the future might use the Light and make legends of their own. So, at the very end of his life, he laid down laws to forbid any other fisherman to even approach the Vortiss.

He had long communicated with a few chosen fisherfolk on shore, using a secret form of writing. Those followers set out the lore of the fishers of Eerie-on-Sea, and Dismal died on his throne, alone, clutching the bottle. And here he would have remained in secret if I hadn't started asking questions. Anyway, it's all here, in his writings."

Squint waves his hand at the recess wall, behind the throne. The rock is covered in words, in tiny, carefully scratched letters.

"Eerie Script!" says Violet, touching the symbols with her hand.

"Know about that, do you?" Old Squint looks impressed.

"A little," says Vi, giving me a wink.

Then Squint leads us back down the rocky steps to the cavern floor.

Where we see something creeping towards us.

CLERMIT

"HERBIE, LOOK!" SAYS VIOLET, pointing at the creeping thing. "Oh, no!"

"Oh, yes!" I cry, overjoyed.

Clambering over tufts and mossy knolls, a mechanical creature I recognize all too well scuttles towards us on four little brass legs.

"Clermit!"

"What?" Violet frowns.

"Clermit," I explain as the wind-up shell gets closer. "'Cl-' from *clockwork* and '-ermit' from *hermit*. Well, I have to call him something, and 'clockwork hermit crab' is a bit of a mouthful. He's back!"

"But ... but I thought it was Deep Hood's gadget."

"Deep Hood had him," I say, "but I don't think

Clermit was ever really his to have. Besides, he's chosen a new home now."

I crouch down, and Clermit comes to a halt beside me. He's got something dangling from one sword arm.

It's my Lost-and-Founder's cap.

I take the cap and put it on, and I feel good as the elastic slides around my chin.

Then I reach down, and Clermit climbs sluggishly into my hands. The brass legs and appendages, gritty with salt and sand, fold slowly into the shell. The whirring of the mechanism *click-click-clicks* to silence as the spring finally unwinds and the shell goes still.

"I made a promise to you," I say, brushing sand and seaweed from the shell with my cuff. "And I'll keep it. I'll find *your* rightful owner, too, one day."

I pop the sleeping Clermit under my cap. Well, I've got used to keeping something there, haven't I?

"I reckon it's time for you two to go home," says old Squint.

"OK," says Vi. "Only I don't have the faintest idea how we do that."

"Ah," he replies with a wink, "there's one more secret I can show you."

Squint Westerley leads us back towards the churning

lake. There is a channel leading out of it, along which shoots a fierce flow of water.

"This is where the water sucked down by the Vortiss finds its way back to the sea. It's the quickest way out." Then he adds, no doubt seeing the alarm on our faces, "It's said there's a route up to the town through caves and fissures at the back of the cavern, but no one – not even Dismal himself – has been able to map the way. Eerie Rock has more holes in it than Swiss cheese, even with Gancy filling up the biggest of them. You'll have to go back the soggy way, I'm afraid. Blaze will pick you up. Don't worry."

"If he's still up there," I say, the squeak creeping back into my voice as I contemplate what's about to happen.

"He'll be there," old Squint declares. "But you'll need this."

He hands Violet his flare gun. She pushes it into her belt.

"And a barrel," Squint adds as he rolls an old barrel towards us.

"Get this over the pair of you, and prepare for the ride of your lives across the bottom of the sea!"

"But won't it be cold?" I say. "Won't it be dark?"

"It'll be a bit bumpy," Squint concedes, "and there are

a few squids and spider crabs. But keep the barrel over you, and the air trapped inside, and you'll soon reach the surface. There's a strong countercurrent that will take you halfway back to Eerie."

Then old Squint puts his fingers to his mouth and whistles an eerie whistle. A nearby sprightning – one of the smaller ones, from the swarm – swoops over, and Squint whispers something we can't catch. It comes and flits around above us.

"This little fellow will give you light."

I look at the tiny electrical creature. It's so like the one I kept under my cap, and yet it *is* different – smaller, less like a fairy, more like a bee.

"Aren't you coming too?" Violet says to Squint.

Old Squint Westerley nods over his shoulder, to where the fishermen of Eerie-on-Sea, with Boadicea Bates, are standing on the shore of the lake, picking up shipwrecked objects and gazing around in wonder.

"Aye, in a few days," he says. "I've got things to show that lot first. And things to say. But we'll be back soon enough, never fear."

So now there's nothing left to do but climb into the rushing water. Squint tips up the barrel and lowers it as gently as he can over us, sprightning and all.

"Ready?" says Violet, beside me in the barrel, icy water up to her shoulders. Her eyes are flashing with excitement.

"*Gng!*" I reply, pressing against the sides of the barrel with my palms to keep myself as wedged as I can.

The sprightning fizzes and crackles.

Then we're off.

How long the journey takes, I cannot say. I have some memory of Violet shrieking with fear, though I suspect it might have actually been delight. There is a really bumpy bit, and the barrel threatens to turn over many times, but then we're rising, suddenly, like a cork, until …

BOOSH!

We hit the surface.

And throw off the barrel.

So now here we are – two bedraggled friends, soaked through and cold, bobbing in the ocean with a tiny sprightning flitting above us. In its fizzing light we see a low, broken rock – one of the sea stacks that has collapsed in the recent earthquakes. We clamber onto it, gasping. Then the sprightning flies away, back towards the Vortiss.

But not before I glimpse Violet holding the flare gun in the air.

PAM!

She fires it.

FZZZZ-zzz-zzz...

The flare rises into the sky.

Brilliant orange light illuminates the choppy sea all around.

"Do you think Blaze really is out here somewhere?" I ask. "His battery was getting flat the last time we saw it. And that must have been hours ago."

Before Violet can answer, I spy a small light on the horizon. We watch as the light grows bigger and bigger, and soon we can see the smashed wheelhouse of the *Jornty Spark* and Blaze Westerley's beaming freckled face, lit by the blue light of the dials.

"Ahoy!" he calls, waving his skipper's cap. "Ahoy there!"

And so it is that we climb aboard the little boat once more, wrap ourselves in oily towels and the warmth of old Squint's engine – not to mention the purrs of Erwin the cat – and watch as Blaze turns the wheel and sets course for home.

"Thirty per cent!" I say, looking at the dial. "But

that's more than when we got swept overboard."

"I rigged up a small waterwheel," Blaze explains. "Using a spare turbine and some bits and bobs. It kept the battery topped up."

"When you see your uncle next," says Vi, "make sure you tell him that. Or I will!"

"You mean...?" Blaze's eyes light up. "You mean, you've seen him? He's *alive*?"

"He is," says Violet.

And she launches into a breathless account of everything we saw down in the undersea cavern, as Blaze blinks in amazement and the *Jornty Spark* carries us home to Eerie-on-Sea.

HERBIE'S CHOICE

IT'S THE NEXT MORNING, and the sky over the bay is clearer than it has been for days. A gentle sun shines low on the horizon, and a clean, crisp wind blows from the sea. It feels like the calm after a storm, which it is. And it feels like the winter has finally ended.

Violet and I arrive early at Seegol's, with Erwin close behind.

"Will you tell them straightaway?" Vi asks me. "Or after chips?"

"Straightaway," I reply, and push open the door.

Seegol's Diner has not escaped the impact of the storm any more than the rest of the town. Several windows are broken, and the building has picked up a bend in its ceiling that it didn't have before.

"Ah!" cries Seegol, beaming at us as he finishes hammering a board over a crack. "You are my first customers of the day. Please, take any seat you like."

We sit at a table in the middle of the diner where the sun shines in cheery squares on the salt shakers and vinegar pots. I'm carrying an enormous bag, so I'm glad to put it down.

"Do you think they'll get here soon?" I say to Vi.

The door of the diner opens, answering my question.

"Hallooo, my dears!" calls a cheery voice. "Hallooo, Mr Seegol! Isn't it lovely out? And such wonderful things to find on the beach today! No time like after a storm for beachcombing."

And Mrs Fossil comes breezing in, carrying a basket. Behind her is Jenny Hanniver.

"It's not every day I'm summoned somewhere," Mrs Fossil continues, settling down at our table and removing a few of her hats. "How exciting!"

"It's for important Lost-and-Founder business," I say, pulling the front of my uniform flat.

"Oh, I'm sure." Jenny smiles. "Thank you for inviting me, too."

"We're just waiting for Dr Thalassi," says Vi. "I can see him coming now."

Sure enough, the doc is striding towards us along the pier, carrying his big black medical bag. His bow tie is crooked, and he looks as if he could do with a sit-down.

"Sorry I'm late," he puffs as he enters the diner. "I have been rushed off my feet. A lot of people were hurt in the storm, and I've just spent the last hour with Lady Kraken. She is displaying some extraordinary symptoms."

Violet and I exchange glances.

"What sort of symptoms?"

"A tiny tentacle!" says Dr Thalassi, putting his bag down. "Or something that looks a lot like one, growing on her back. And she claims to have been able to walk again for a few hours, which is quite impossible with her condition. But she's very excited. She kept asking me about something called an 'ocean potion', though I don't approve of these alternative remedies myself. Oh, and she told me to tell you, Herbie, that she's expecting a full report later today. I believe the word she used to describe you was 'dunderbrain'."

I do a slightly desperate grin.

"Anyway," the doc continues, "her 'tentacle' is already showing signs of dropping off, so I prescribed her an ointment. I expect it will be gone in a day or two."

"Thank you, all, for coming," I say then, standing up

and feeling nervous about being the centre of attention. "I'm pleased to say that I have finished my investigation into The Case of the Fish-Shaped Bottle, and I've summoned you all to hear what I've decided to do about it, and then to eat a huge slap-up lunch of fish and chips and whatever it is Mrs Fossil has brought with her in that basket, though I'm hoping it's muffins."

"It is!" declares Mrs F.

I reach into my bag and heave out the empty fish-shaped bottle, and with help from Violet, manage to get it into the centre of the table. It gleams at us with aqua light and ancient mystery.

"My lovely beachcombing find!" gasps Mrs Fossil. "So beautiful."

"My historical artefact!" says the doc, letting his specs fall over his nose. "Quite fascinating."

"So, what have you decided, Herbie?" says Jenny.

"I have decided," I say, "that the rightful owner of this bottle is Mrs Fossil. She found it. It belongs to her."

"OOH!" Mrs Fossil claps her hands.

Dr Thalassi falls silent. He looks down at the Formica tabletop, defeated.

"Oh, Doc, don't take it like that," cries Mrs F, her triumph evaporating as soon as she sees his face. "Please don't be sad. There's only one bottle, and we can't cut it in two. Oh, why does it have to be so tricky!"

Violet coughs a little "ahem" cough.

"Well, you could *donate* your bottle to the museum," she says. "You would still be the official finder and owner, of course. Your name would be on the card beside the bottle, explaining it all and telling visitors to the museum where they can find your wonderful Flotsamporium, as well as Eerie-on-Sea's most famous beachcomber."

"Famous?" says Mrs Fossil.

"And then," I say, taking over from Violet, "in your shop window, you could display a framed photo of you with the bottle – along with a card explaining it all, and telling visitors to your Flotsamporium where they can find the amazing Museum of Eerie, and its distinguished curator."

Dr Thalassi straightens his bow tie.

"Yes," says Mrs Fossil, looking into the distance and considering. "Yes, I could do that. And I could come to see the bottle whenever I wanted…"

"I would display it at the museum entrance, in pride of place," says the doc quickly. "It would be the first thing people see when they enter, Wendy. I promise you that."

"Then I agree," declares Wendy Fossil, flashing her

snaggletooth grin and shaking hands with the delighted doc. "No, don't try to stop me! It's my bottle, and I'll donate it if I want to."

"Thank you, Mrs Fossil," says Dr Thalassi.

Violet and I do a fist bump, discreetly, under the table.

"That means that the museum will have another example of Eerie Script to add to the collection," the doctor continues. "If you are still interested in the secret letters, Violet, come over with Herbie for those lessons, and we can examine them. Who knows, you may even help me make a breakthrough!"

The doc chuckles at that last bit, as if the idea is preposterous.

I look at Violet and see that she's smiling sweetly and saying thanks. But I also see a fierce light in her eyes that tells me she can't wait to get to the museum and start translating the code in front of Dr Thalassi. I *definitely* want to be there for that.

"Fish and chips almost ready," says Mr Seegol, coming to join us, the thumb of one hand tucked proudly in his apron string while the fingers of his other are miraculously hooked around the necks of six bottles of chilled lemonade.

"Maybe you can all help me with something first,"

says Vi, pulling a book from her coat pocket.

She places it on the table.

And there, despite the sun and the warmth and the promise of the day, lies a horrible sight that chills me to the bone:

The
COLD, DARK
BOTTOM
of the
SEA
by
SEBASTIAN
EELS

On the cover, the stricken liner is eternally sinking beside its iceberg, while underwater the drowning passengers writhe and twist as they fall to the depths. From the lower edge, tentacles, claws and feelers reach up to snatch them for ever.

The mood around the table changes.

"Why have you brought *that*, Violet?" Jenny Hanniver demands. "I was just beginning to feel summery."

"The mermonkey dispensed it," Violet says, avoiding my eye but catching everyone else's. "I just wondered what you all thought. If it was dispensed to you, I mean. What would you think it meant?"

"Ah," says Seegol. "I've read this novel. I would just see it as a reminder of where the fish I serve come from. Nothing more."

"A rather simple interpretation," sniffs Dr Thalassi. "But understandable. For me it would be a sign that death will come to us all one day, whether you're a rich passenger at the captain's table or a lowly dishwasher in the ship's galley."

"Trust you to think of something gloomy like that!" declares Mrs Fossil. "For me it would mean: make the most of life while you can. Sing! Beachcomb! Make tea for your friends and bake cakes! Maybe spend a bit less time curating – and a bit more time having fun."

Everyone laughs at that. Well, almost everyone. Jenny Hanniver is looking at the book in silence. Then she turns to me.

"I'd like to know what Herbie thinks."

Everyone turns to me.

"I think…" I start to say. "I think that maybe…"

And I wonder – wonder about the things Sebastian Eels said to me in the cave. Is the sinking of the SS *Fabulous* actually a true story? Did Eerie-on-Sea's most famous author *steal* the idea from real events, and pass it off as his own work of fiction? Is there hope for me in *The Cold,*

Dark Bottom of the Sea, after all? And suddenly, as I look again at the disturbing cover art, I see something that I never noticed before: on the white line that represents the surface of the sea, there are little shapes. I'd always thought they were just distant icebergs, floating in the ocean, but now – as the sunlight of a new day streams down onto the book – I understand what they really are.

Lifeboats. Rowing away from disaster.

Full of survivors.

Could my parents be among them?

"Herbie?" says Violet, cutting through my thoughts.

"I think," I say, blinking with the possibilities of it all, "that maybe, in the end, it doesn't really matter what horrible things happened to me in the past, or what the future may bring, because today, here and now, with all my friends around me, I reckon Seegol's chips will taste better than they've ever tasted. But not if we let them get cold."

Jenny Hanniver picks up the book and hands it over to me.

"I think that's *exactly* what it means," she says with a smile. I do a grin in reply as I slip the book into my pocket.

Then the chips arrive, and drinks are poured, and a

lunch fit for the king of the merfolk is spread out before us on the table.

"I hope you don't mind that I brought that book," Vi says later, while everyone is chatting. "But it is my job."

"As assistant at the Eerie Book Dispensary?"

"As your *best friend*," she replies, slipping another fish-cake to Erwin under the table. "There are always a hundred different ways to feel about the books the mermonkey dispenses, even one written by Sebastian Eels."

"A book is like a mirror," I reply, watching Erwin licking his chops. "We always see ourselves inside."

The cat winks at me with one of his ice-blue eyes, but says nothing.

"Yes," says Violet. "And now we know Sebastian Eels knew something about your past when he wrote *The Cold, Dark Bottom of the Sea*, we can read the book and look for *clues*, Herbie. Clues about your past we can *research*! Maybe we'll even find a passenger list for the SS *Fabulous*! And *then*... Hey, Herbie? Are you listening to me?"

I am. But I don't have anything else to say right now.

Because Violet's entirely right.

And I'm already eating a muffin.

THOMAS TAYLOR has always lived near the sea (though that's not difficult in the British Isles). He comes from a long line of seafarers but chose a career as an illustrator because that involves less getting wet and better biscuits.

His first professional illustration commission, straight out of art school, was the cover art for *Harry Potter and the Philosopher's Stone*. This led to a lot more drawing until he finally plucked up the courage to try writing for himself. It turns out that turning biscuits into books is even more fun when you get to create the story, too.

Thomas currently lives on the south coast of England, which provided a lot of the weather for this book. As a keen beachcomber he has found several messages in bottles over the years, including one that appeared to be in secret code. He hasn't been struck by lightning yet, but as the best time to find beachcombing treasures is just after a storm, it's surely only a matter of time.